OTHER BOOKS BY JEFFREY LEWIS

Meritocracy: A Love Story

THE CONFERENCE
of
THE BIRDS

A NOVEL

THE CONFERENCE
of
THE BIRDS

A NOVEL BY

JEFFREY LEWIS

Other Press · New York

Copyright © 2005 Jeffrey Lewis

Production Editor: Mira S. Park
Book design by Natalya Balnova

This book was set in 11 pt. A Caslon by Alpha Graphics of Pittsfield, NH.

10 9 8 7 6 5 4 3 2 1

ISBN 1-59051-124-7
A CIP for this title is available from the Library of Congress.

Publisher's Note: This is a work of fiction. Names, characters, places, and incidents either are the product of the author's imagination or are used fictitiously, and any resemblance to actual persons, living or dead, events, or locales is entirely coincidental.

for Rick

CHAPTER 1

THE WINDOW IS DIRTY. Soot has mottled it so that it resembles a topographical map of a region of hills. Rain has caused the soot to run in places, creating rivers or gullies. Raindrops themselves, bearers of the city's detritus, have left faint pockmarks, as though long ago a war had been fought here. Shelling. Death. Verdun. The Western Front. One's imagination could run wild. Don't. Stop. Go back. Nothing wild here. Wild is the city, the world, the wind. Here is cultivation. Here is human possibility. Go back. Stop. Gently, so that even "human possibility" is stopped, so that even stopping is stopped.

The landscape of war is deposited on the window's outside. On the pane's inside, particles of dust and faint angular streaks where some window washer years ago used a dirty squeegee. Also, dapples of grease, like settling mist, as though grease has been in the air of the place.

I reach for a scrap of torn-up newspaper. I feel the air rustle against the insides of my fingers as I extend my arm. I feel my fingertips as they land, gentle as a mosquito on skin, on the pile of newsprint squares. My thumb and two fingers pinch the top sheet, which like something hypnotized slides into their grip. Gently, cautiously, they lift the single sheet. With any less pressure it would flutter away. My right arm reaches for the bottle of window cleaner. The solution is pale, diluted, watery. One doesn't waste Windex just as one doesn't waste newspaper. There's no need. Need is elsewhere. Need is a poem, or need has no name. Stop. Gently. Go back.

Sense my arms and legs. Look. Listen.

The muffled boogie-woogie of the taxi honks, ten stories down. The creak of floorboards as they're stepped on. No voices. No music. Somewhere the low beating of a helicopter's heart, becoming stronger, then receding. I press my finger down on the Windex pump. The flesh of my finger flattens against the concave plastic of the pump, the pump emits a snorting sound, then the splat of the cleaner on the window. I squirt again. I squirt until the entire window is laced with drips. Have I squirted too much? In my inattention did I press too hard? Stop. Don't bother. Go back. Sense my arms and legs.

Words, that's the point, everywhere words, words for everything. I drown in words. I struggle to keep my head up. Stop. Go back. Gently float as mild as Ivory soap ninety-nine and forty-four hundredths percent pure but that isn't pure enough. Why isn't it pure enough? Why does everything have to be pure? What's the point? Who says?

Stop. Go back. Sense. Look. Listen.

Nothing more.

The window cleaner dribbles down the pane, tears on a ravaged face whose sorrow I arrest with my slip of newsprint. As lightly as I can, so that I can sense the resistance of the wet glass to the paper,

I make rounding motions with my arm and swirl the cleaner around the window. I continue to rub. I sense the cleaner loosening the grease, I sense the newsprint absorbing the liquefied grime. I rub but also I glide. I'm like a skater on this pane of glass.

What time is it? I lift my left wrist to look at my watch. Twenty after seven. Only twenty minutes gone. I have to do this until nine o'clock.

I could sink into time. I could arrest time. I could cause clocks to slow.

Stop. Imagination. Go back.

Clocks are already slow.

Fuck this shit this made-up shit why am I here why don't I walk out of here?

The window sticks when I try to raise it, to bring the top window down, to make an exchange of windows. I press with the bottoms of my palms on the inside frame, my neck and jaw and shoulders tense, the window flies up on its ropes, and only then do I realize how many unnecessary muscles I've brought to bear, and begin to relax them.

The top window is divided into six panes. I will squirt them, rub them, clean them one at a time. Space can expand or contract. Time can slow or race. It's only a matter of attention, or would the psychologists call it perception? And am I spouting merely metaphor? And anyway stop, go back, gently.

I must move my attention to my arms and legs and to listening and looking.

Six panes. One pane at a time. More squares of newsprint. More squirts.

Now it's seven forty-five. Joyous thought. Am I looking at my watch again? This is easy, it seems to say, just wash the windows and don't think and I'll watch your life tick by and soon enough . . .

nine o'clock? The sweat under the leather strap of the watch. Its round and friendly face. Is it time to take a break? I'm almost out of paper squares. This too is reason for joy, that now I'll have to walk across the room to the stack of newspaper in the broom closet. It's like a prisoner's walk in the yard. Life is sweet. The colors of Laura's clothes her breasts the carpet Cal washing the windows next to me Bobby peeling the paper off garlic dumping bok choy in the wok Julie pretty Julie her mouth slightly open her jaw slack with woozy extended motions sanding a table leg. Joe like the Little King in his corduroy pants with the elastic waistband walking around saying nothing. I bring a section of newspaper back to my window. The paper is months old. Classified ads for boats. I ignore this, I try to ignore this, I try to ignore the other pages as well. Don't try, do.

I lift the window with pliant fingertips. I turn around and seat myself on the sill as if I'm about to eject from an aircraft and slide on my pant legs over the uneven edges of the sill until I'm outside facing back into the loft. I can see the galley, the clamp lights, the particle board furniture, Joe's miniature roses under their Gro-lites, as if I were spying into a stranger's home. I lower the window until its frame rests on my thighs, my calves dangling inside as if held ransom for my safe return. I breathe the chill night air. My abdomen tightens. I tell myself to breathe. I tell myself not to tell myself anything at all.

I begin again to wash the window. I do not focus on the color, the movement, or the humanity inside the loft. I do not focus on being ten stories up and the possibilities that if the window broke or I got stupid or a pigeon shat on my head I might fall. I focus on the topography of grime. What time is it now? Yes, I am afraid to die. Yes, I am proud to be out on this sill. I am better than earth dwellers. I am part of a merry band my heart beats lightly I cannot die not now not like this why would I?

I love life down to its atoms. When have I ever thought that before? Stop. Go back. Look at my watch don't look at my watch don't start that shit again.

But time is slow. This could go on forever. When will it be over?

I see Bobby in the galley. Slender Bobby with his curly dark hair and no smile just now as his wrist flicks the knife and the scallions go down in a chopped heap like he was a G-man riddling a pack of John Dillingers. A quarter past eight. Still three-quarters of an hour to go. I descend into the Land of Window. I tell stories of this Land. I'm tiring. I should take a break. Yes, I'll take a break. Out on this ledge I take a break. I don't wash. I look up and see that the moon is out, a half-moon, sickly, between buildings.

In the Land of Window there are mountains and streams. In the Land of Window there is paint in the corners. Send in the troops, get this thing cleaned up.

Why is everything I do accompanied by words?

What happened to my joy in possibility? So recent I could taste it but I'm totally crazy now, my mind flies around.

I forget about the paint in the corners. Or rather, I move my attention away from it.

A conscious act not an unconscious act.

Oh yeah who says I'll be the judge of that says who.

I raise the window. I gather up my stack of unused newsprint and the used, dirty squares of paper and the window cleaner and I duck back inside. I feel a measure of warmth and safety in my throat and behind my eyes.

Now the window looks beautiful. Between outside and inside a veil has been lifted.

O prideful one, O bullshit artist calm down, don't you see, calm down. Go back. You know the drill.

If you can't see the window at all, that's when you've got a window. If a bird could fly into it.

I look at my watch again. Eight thirty-five. In the loft, here and there, others sit and smoke cigarettes, their feet flat on the floor, the smoke inhaled and exhaled in easy, attenuated drafts like the coming and going of a sea on a flat beach. I could take a break again but I just took one.

I must wash a second window. I have time. There's no excuse. The thought sickens me. Wasn't one plenty? I did so well, got it so clean. You lazy swine what better have you got to do go pick up girls uptown in bars, long for girls in bars on Broadway? And yet if I am deceived? And yet if we are all deceived? We birds of desire we birds of longing dirty New York birds with doubts in our heads.

What is life worth except to be impeccable? A clean window, something more than I'd done before.

Wash the window and dirty more paper and tear more paper and rub and swirl and cleanse and dry and quiet my mind.

And then, like life or so they say, a bout of amnesia and it's almost over. Five to nine. Clean up. Put the window cleaner and the unused paper back in the broom closet. Cal does it too. I'm not alone. I'm not the first. I'm jumping no guns.

Everyone put to sleep, waking up with regret, nostalgia, forgetfulness. Waking up just before the end.

I tell myself I did it. I actually feel quite strong. The work is humble but the work is real, it is the work of waking up is it not?

Go back. Sense.

Stop all the other nonsense including the nonsense of stopping the nonsense and the nonsense of talking about the nonsense of stopping the nonsense and so on in endless recessional.

Go back. Sense.

The meeting is short. Scarcely anyone has anything to say. We sit on pine benches or on the floor in front of them. A few lonesome, venturing voices. "I was finding it hard to sense tonight." "A lot of anger kept coming up about my sister." "I felt this sensation in my chest, like it was almost burning." Offerings of a sort, expressions of hope, of ongoingness, or fear. Joe says nothing. Joe sits in his Eames chair. His watery gray eyes moving around, avoiding people's glances. Now, dinner. A single lamb chop on a bed of greens, a shot of iced vodka. "Damn the torpedoes! Full speed ahead!" Joe's perennial toast. The pine benches in a square. Bobby and Julie serving. I throw my vodka back. It burns, a pledge, a confirmation. Are we not men, Devo said and we say it too. The bloody juice of the lamb, salty and slightly fragrant on my tongue. My teeth grind slowly, sacramentally. The flesh of the lamb gives way. I swallow and wonder how. The shadows of words even on this bench. Silence now. Plates collected, piled one on top of another with short ceramic claps. Sense. Look. Listen. Joe smoking a cigarette. Now a dozen others smoke and the smoke lingers over us all as if a reminder of the sea of air we swim in. Abdomens relax. Breathe deep. Sense. When will this silence be over? Is not enough enough? Has the vodka made me drunk?

I will be happy to be out of here. I will be happy to be out in the world. I've done as much as I can.

My ass begins to ache. Bony ass on the pine bench. My wallet in my pants doesn't help. What's it doing there, so asymmetric? I fidget. I straighten my spine. I lift my weight slightly onto my feet to give my ass a break.

Joe butts his Newport out. He has a face like a stone wall. Silence as a reminder, or a goal, or an enemy. I'd like to tear it to bits. When. When. When. Sense. Look. Listen. "That's all for tonight," Joe says, and rubs his cigarette butt around in his ashtray.

I rise. It's over. No one says another word.

At the elevator people's shoes are scattered around. It looks like a haphazard parking lot of shoes. I find my old loafers, dirty, their leather cracked and split apart. I slip them on. My feet feel like they've entered a womb.

The elevator arrives. I'll be in the first batch down. But before anyone goes anywhere, Joe shouts as if it were an afterthought, "The week between Christmas and New Year's, don't anybody fly to Rio! We're having an event!"

His voice bright and hortatory, for a moment the voice of a cheerleader.

I know the word "event." My heart sinks faster than the elevator down. We've had weekend events, working night and day from Friday evening through Sunday. But an event for an entire week?

Go back. Calm down. Sense. No one says anything in the elevator. It's one of the things, no talking till you're in the street. Things to gather and save attention. On the street we say nothing either. We walk in our separate directions.

I hate Joe now. I hate his jaunty tone. A whole week without sleep, without escape, a whole week of . . . what?

Is that what he said, a week? Or did he mean, an event *sometime during* the week, two days perhaps?

No I know what he meant. No doubt in my black heart. I can't do a whole week of this, I'll lose my mind, or isn't that the point?

Go back. Gently. Sense. Look. Listen.

Broadway. Wind whipping the trash. A few bums, a few kids. Street smells of ozone and exhaust and broken bags of garbage. I renew my conscious effort to see and this world of disorder becomes fixed and composed, as if captured in a time elapse photo. Ribbons of taxis.

I wait for the train at Broadway-Lafayette. I catch the D and ride uptown. People on the train read the paper, spread out, find warmth in hooded sweatshirts. I begin to feel superior to these ordinary lives, worried about this or that. I watch a woman with a careworn face as if to correct myself. All my life have I not found some way to feel superior to someone? Are people telling me I'm crazy? Sense. Look. Listen.

At 59th Street where I change trains there's a homeless guy on the floor who asks for change. I look at him and think of the stories of gods or holy men who've gone in disguise to test the nature of man, and for this reason alone, no other, I reach into my pants and throw a quarter at him. It lands on his leg and skitters off. It rolls on its edge on the floor until it's out of his reach. I think what the fuck, in for a penny in for a pound, and lean over and pick up the quarter and put it in his hand. The backs of my fingernails brush against the roughness of his palm. The homeless guy mutters "bless you." For a moment I hate myself with all my heart and even that feels like a lie.

I change for the IRT and continue uptown to home.

CHAPTER 2

JOE SOMETIMES READ ALOUD the story of the Greek and Chinese artists. The emperor of Persia offered a contest: whoever proved themselves to be the greatest artists would win a valuable commission. A delegation came from China, another from Greece. The Chinese artists, who brought with them rich pigments, the finest brushes, rare papers, set to work at once with great skill and soon produced a magnificent painting. For vibrancy of color and delicacy of figure and line, none had seen its like. The emperor declared it to be the most beautiful work of art he had ever seen. The Persian court little doubted that the Chinese would take the prize. Meanwhile no one had seen what the Greeks were working on. All that they did, they did in secret. When at last they unveiled their achievement, people were first bewildered. It was nothing more than a cleansed and polished mirror. But when the Chinese painting was reflected in it, it appeared even more glorious and beautiful than before. It shone in perfect splendor, as did all the rest of creation. The Greeks were awarded the commission, for, declared the emperor, they had most truly held a mirror to life.

*

We had no name. We were simply "the group."

*

In *The Conference of the Birds*, a twelfth century poem by Attar, thirty birds set out on a perilous journey to reach the mighty Simurgh, whose name means thirty birds. Is that who we were?

Starling and pet shop parakeet and sparrow and seagull and crow.

The Hoopoe, who was a guide to King Solomon, who obtained a crown of glory, was their guide, urging them on, defeating their excuses, giving them hope.

*

Was the Hoopoe too fancy a bird for Joe? He who said he was "just another kike from Brooklyn."

*

Sometime in July of 1974 I went on a Thursday evening to the apartment of Philip Deschayne on 13th Street in the Village. I was brought there by a friend of a college friend, a woman named Joan Dreyfus. Joan was unclear exactly what was going on in Philip's apartment, but whatever it was was vaguely "literary" and open to the public. At the time I had not expected the world to ignore me so completely. The fact that Philip wrote for the *New Yorker* enticed me. We entered a small back apartment in a townhouse. An assortment of books lay in a pile on the living room carpet, surrounded by a half-dozen people who sat in a rough circle almost in reach of them. Philip told us to pull up a chair. Thin and tall with sunken cheeks and a boyish sweep of dark hair, clear plastic prep school glasses, he had, I thought, an unusually intense gaze. He was willing to stare at a stranger. At the same time his manner was pleasant. Others present included a guy in an ascot with a hawkish nose, a slight dark-eyed kid in his early twenties, and a girl with saucery glasses and orange frizzy hair, a face like a lollipop. At the last moment a man with the proportions if not the full size of a defensive lineman walked in, stood behind the couch, removed a trench coat. He had bulldoggy jowls and a notably immobile expression—not mean or scowling, simply immobile—that I remember at the time thinking contrasted oddly with his boyish freckles, as though you were looking at both man and boy at once. He may have been in his mid-thirties. The books were full of stories. People were free to pick them up, peruse them, and if a story struck them somehow, read it aloud. This was how things appeared to me, anyway. I couldn't tell a pattern to what was read, except that all the stories seemed "oriental." Several were humorous, others seemed quite beautiful. The entire impression the evening made was of quiet and an esthetically pleasing purity. The last story was read by the heavy-set man with the jowls and freckles, and it ended with an offer of a few dates to a needy person. Philip Deschayne then passed around a small plate of dates. I returned to his apartment the following Thursday. Joan Dreyfus did not. I presumed the stories, or the company, were not to her liking. Afterwards I began having small conversations with other participants, particularly the kid, Bobby Gelfand, a cartoonist who'd dropped out of Harvard after painting a lamppost on Mount Auburn Street with the 100 Greatest Hits from the Hundred Years' War. I remembered the painted lamppost from my time in law school, its stick-figure drollery, its stark hysteria. The second time I went to Philip Deschayne's, I read a story out loud. I didn't know why I was doing it. I liked the story. I thought it might show my good taste. I wanted to have new friends. I had chosen to be a writer, I was stuck in my room, and here seemed to be my people. After the third week, Bobby said to me that if I wanted to find out a little more, I could go to another apartment, on Charles Street, on Saturday afternoon. The second apartment belonged to Joe, the heavy-set guy who had by then made a firm impression on me for being the last to read each Thursday evening. When I arrived, Bobby and Philip were both there, as was the frizzy-haired girl, Liddie. They were each painting a section of a lime green wall with what seemed to be obsessive care. They were moving so slowly, it was as if some drug had slowed their metabolism. Joe was efficient and nonplused. There was nothing slowed about his movements. He asked me if I would like to try this. He was friendly enough. I tried to gauge if I could still come on Thursday nights to Philip's and read stories if I declined. I guessed that I could but that I would be a second-class citizen. I wanted to know what was going on, I wanted to be a part. I said sure, why not. He told me to sit in a chair and to shut my eyes and then, in a tone of voice similar to the one in which he read stories, that is to say, very clearly, very declaratively, as though making a deliberate effort to avoid imparting to his words any sort of emotional coloration, he gave me a certain mental exercise to do. He told me to repeat the exercise each morning shortly after I woke up. He told me not to reveal the exercise to anyone unless I consulted him first, because they might not know what to do with it, by which I thought he meant they might be harmed by it. When I opened my eyes, Joe told me to do my best to sense my arms and legs and look and listen, and if I became aware of being distracted, by words or pictures in my head, to go back to sensing, looking and listening. I could do this all the time, he said, day and night, but I should begin now, in the apartment, painting a section of wall. Afterwards, he said, we could talk about how it went.

*

Four years passed.

CHAPTER 3

WHENEVER I SAW BOBBY with Joe, I was aware of the watch.
A Casio that sold at Bondy's on Division Street for eighty or ninety
dollars, with a stainless steel band that reminded me of a high school
ID bracelet and digital readouts as though the future had arrived and
it was all about putting things in neat rectangular boxes. Both wore
the same watch, but on Joe it seemed to fit, with his elasticized pants
and engineer's short-sleeve shirts, whereas on Bobby's narrow wrist
it looked outsized and imposed, as though he'd decided to hype his
masculinity or a salesman had sold him on that idea. But Bobby was
masculine enough. And one of the few certainties I felt about Joe
was that he had lousy taste in clothes, Sears Roebuck taste in clothes.
Bobby's Casio watch on his wrist felt to me like the black choker
Julie Christie wore in a film once, to suggest she was the possession
of some man.

Though Philip had a Casio, too, and I had a Seiko that I wore
for awhile then put away in my drawer. We all imitated Joe in ways

large and small. I told myself it was certainly not in adoration and probably not even in admiration but rather an experiment, to try to see what Joe was like, or rather, by seeing what Joe was like who hypothetically had the goods on self-discovery, to see what we were like. We were becoming Joe in order to become ourselves. Yet when I saw Bobby wearing that watch, I felt embarrassed by it. It was in such pathetic bad taste. "Just a kike from Bensonhurst." I didn't want us to be from Bensonhurst. I wanted us to be from Harvard and Yale. Although he never said it, I assumed it must be part of Joe's program to knock Harvard and Yale out of us.

For were these elite universities not part of our conditioning, too, the part that allowed us to feel special and superior and kept our minds busy with fantasies and divided us from ourselves? This much, in time, I came seriously to consider.

Though "considering," also, was not a part of what we were supposed to be doing, and anyway not all of us had gone to Harvard or Yale. Philip had gone to Harvard, and Cal Bittker, and Bobby dropped out and Ty Duncan was on the *Lampoon* there and I went to Yale, and Valerie worked at Sotheby's and fucked guys who had gone to Harvard. But most of the rest of us Joe found through an ad in the *Voice*. I never knew what the ad said. I didn't really want to know, though I imagined it must have been something like "Are you interested in understanding yourself?" Something overripe with patent medicine promise, or just bizarre and vague enough that if I'd read it myself I'd not have given it a second thought. Yet the ad attracted filings from every sort of New York life, bond salesmen and musicians and secretaries and con men. Or to go back to the old metaphor: birds of every plumage flew in through the window, the variety of birds you find in a city, not least among them quite ordinary pigeons.

I had just done my bit for Thanksgiving at Astor Liquor. As if the gleaming glass alone could stupefy me, I'd stood paralyzed in the aisle of vodka bottles for twenty minutes, taking one bottle off the shelf then another. Twice I got to the checkout counter with half a dozen bottles in my cart and turned around. To buy the cheap shit, the house brand, or only the best or something in-between. Arguments crowding my mind. My relative poverty, my civil servant salary, the difficulty for the average consumer of telling one vodka from another but were these really average consumers and was it going in a punch or would it be drunk neat? I tried to distinguish the voices in my head. Were these mine, my mother's, my father's, Joe's? Go back, I told myself, stop, it doesn't matter, go back, sense, look. Look at these sleek bottles of vodka in their long row like soldiers. In the end I chose the best. Nothing but the best for Joe, I could not be humiliated if I bought the best, I could not disrespect. A hundred dollars of vodka, half my take-home pay. Why not? Did it not lend a touch of glory to the enterprise, didn't it mean I was in synch? I brought the vodka bottles up to the loft, removed them from the Astor Liquor shopping bag, placed them lovingly one by one on the galley counter as if they were a catch of fourteen-inch trout. Joe padded by but said nothing. He was working on something with the band saw. All right well fuck you then, if you won't even recognize my sacrifice don't you see what I've done. But he didn't, or didn't care to acknowledge, or was just making my life miserable. Sense. Look. Listen. Bobby chopping scallions. He was always here, in the loft, or so it seemed. He had a room somewhere but it must have been airless and tiny, he had even less money than I—every once in a while the *New Yorker* paid him for a couple cartoons and he spent all the money on what? I wasn't sure but on something other than survival. Bobby chopping scallions. The day before Thanksgiving, doing all the prep. Two obscenely white Chinatown toms, stripped and humiliated prisoners, sitting trussed on the counter. I began to chop alongside him. I had often helped him, I was very nearly his apprentice in the galley, I liked the smells and the tastes and the fact I was learning something practical, so that if the whole group went to hell I'd still come out of it knowing how to boil a potato or cure a wok. Bobby had taught me how to chop with easy thrusts of my wrist so that the weight of the knife carried it through the food. With scallions this became almost effortless. No squeezing of the knife, no chops to mar the cutting board, no tensing of any muscles. Kitchen Zen, kitchen ju-jitsu, more miraculous than any late night invention by Popeel. I watched the scallions collapse into little piles of green O's and imagined, like the text of one of Bobby's recent cartoons, which had become more esoteric and less funny and salable, that "from this cook I learned how to take care of my life." Stop it, fuck it, don't be absurd if you're going to do this then do it but don't brag.

And not because bragging was wrong, it was no more wrong than anything else but it didn't get you anywhere—it was one more turn on the wheel.

Though wheels weren't our metaphor. Wheels weren't our deal.

The doorbell from down in the lobby. On the intercom a voice you might imagine coming from a happy piece of sandpaper, animated and jumping around. A woman's voice, nasal also. "I come up? What are you doing? It's Maisie." Joe buzzed her in.

A few moments later, Maisie McLaren got off the elevator, her olive-dyed suede coat, her freckles, blue eyes, round face, her red hair that if it were only longer as I remembered it would have been flying around. Her red hair that was darker than Liddie's, streaked with fire in a way unmatchable by CVS, some throwback to the highlands.

Because I was working for the moment I said nothing to her, nor she to me. Our code of courtesy, our prime rule: don't interfere with another's attention. Don't try to steal another's attention. Crappy little hello's, don't bother, don't pretend they're not little concoctions of neediness or hate. But I knew Maisie from before, not well, really, but I knew her. She was the sister of a woman I once loved and tried more than once to write about. Sascha Maclaren who died in a car crash and I never kissed her once. But she's another story, or maybe she isn't, since Maisie was a friend of Joan Dreyfus who took me to Philip Deschayne's, and so if I hadn't known Maisie and hadn't loved Sascha I could not have felt the sweet scent of scallions marking my breath like colored dye the moment she walked in. Maisie had started Sarah Lawrence but wound up at McLean's, where rich girls went for their nervous breakdowns which in her case may have had to do with Sascha, with her death, or maybe not. After McLean's she'd hung around Cambridge and got involved with a group in Somerville that was run by Joe's old teacher and came up or down with Hodgkin's disease and so she was treated for that and continued with Joe's old teacher and wound up saying, in her throaty voice with her smoker's happy cackle, that it took Hodgkin's to cure her of McLean's.

She was supposed to be better now. I'd heard something about her coming down to the city to hang around Joe for awhile. Joe who himself had beaten testicular cancer, and this was part of his legend too. The doctors had given him a pick-a-number chance, ten percent, twenty percent, but he'd chosen to understand himself or die trying and here he was years later, one ball short but breathing fire.

Joe's legend. "Just another kike from Brooklyn." The pieces Philip wrote in the *New Yorker*. "Our friend from the Pratt Institute." "Our friend Joe."

People always seemed to know one another's names. Either that or it didn't matter and when they needed to they'd know. I say this because it wasn't as if Joe introduced Bobby to Maisie, or that Maisie introduced herself. She stuck around, took off her coat. "Need help with the food?" "Thanks. Nah." "I'm good with pumpkin. I'm good with marshmallows." "Done for today."

He slid the birds into the fridge and looked at her twice.

Bobby who had a childlike smile, a smile you could make a bet on, though I don't remember if he smiled at her then.

Joe came back from the band saw and put *The Thief of Baghdad* in the Betamax. Joe, Maisie, Bobby, myself. It being another portion of the indecipherable puzzle of ourselves that we watched Joe's television as much as we did. Before going to Joe's I hadn't watched TV since I was twelve. But here he was like a boy with his Betamax and his tapes and the biggest Sony you could then buy. And we all went along, sat around. Smoking, sharing the air, not looking at one another but rather at movies we'd seen many times before. Joe treated Bobby like a servant. If Joe wanted a bowl of ice cream, Bobby got it for him. If Joe was out of ice cream, Bobby went to the store. Even with Maisie there, Joe ordered Bobby around. "Jeeves, how 'bout some coffee?" "Jeeves, what's cooking for dinner?" "Jeeves, did you remember to buy cigarettes?" "Shit. I forgot." And Bobby would run off. All of which I understood to be part of Bobby being Joe's most promising pupil, either that or his most problematic case, the one who was so desperate he was ready for all or anything. But why, just now, in front of Maisie? Bobby who seemed as sweet as a baby yet Joe had often said, and Bobby concurred, that he was full of narcissism and loathing. "A power-mad rat." Were we not all power-mad rats? The phrase in vogue, the vernacular phrase. Why else endure such patent abasements except in hopes of grabbing the golden ring?

I felt pity as much as envy for Bobby. But would Maisie understand? Maisie who'd been part of the Boston group, who sat and watched the *Thief* and seemed surprised by nothing.

The old movie with Sabu for the umpteenth time. Has umpteenth become a word yet? Hardly matters because it wasn't really the umpteenth time, more like the fifth, each Thanksgiving Joe brought it out, his favorite film, the little boy hero who just wants to have some fun after he's solved the big world's problems. Joe chattered, rooted, cheered, he was like a kid in a Saturday matinee and everytime the thief was about to get in trouble he'd shout at the screen, "Don't do it! Don't *do* it," singsongy, entirely engaged, as if the next thing he'd start biting his nails. Sabu reminded me of Bobby, his size, his sly charm, his agility. More than a few times I wondered if what drew Joe to Bobby was his resemblance to Sabu, as if in that resemblance he saw a clue to Bobby's possibilities. Joe believed in movies, more than I did, believed in Errol Flynn and Janet Gaynor and names I never knew, all from the forties and thirties, from the time when he was a kid or just before he was born, when his parents were young. As if somehow, in these dreams that must have overarched their lives, or sprung out of them by the populist alchemy of Hollywood's machine, Joe was seeking the romance of his parents' lives, or his own romance when with a kid's inevitable longing he tried to live theirs. Joe's father had a dry cleaners. Joe never talked about him.

Just as none of us talked about our parents but watched the movies of their youth and listened to the Andrews Sisters and a young Bing Crosby and Maurice Chevalier on the scores of tapes that Joe churned out on his dual-cassette deck. We seldom spoke of our parents, seldom visited them or said a kind word about them, but often relived the moments when our parents might have danced or been in love. And Joe got as much pleasure from his cassettes as from his Betamax, singing along, crooning really, like someone who'd once been afraid of the sound of his own voice but gotten over it. "Oh Rio, Rio by the sea, oh." "I'm just a lonely babe in the woods/So lady be good . . ." Though Joe loved the old Apollo too. "Gimme a pigfoot and a bottle of beer . . ."

It was as if he'd secreted a whole other part of himself, maybe the happiest part, in these movies and tunes.

I didn't understand. I couldn't understand. Why try to make words out of something that had no words?

Sense. Look. Listen.

I had to leave for a couple of hours. Work related. Downtown. The D.A.'s office. Where I worked, by the way. Assistant D.A. me. The result of Joe's prodding me to quit writing, get out of my room, get out in the world. "You ought to get a job. Quit driving yourself crazy." Offered as a suggestion, nothing more. Except for Bobby, Joe never ordered anybody to do anything, but I hated him for suggesting it. I had my ninety dollars a week from a one day gig at Columbia. But Joe thought I ought to be more "normal." In truth the D.A. was the first job I could find. Their hunger for Harvard Law grads who would work for fourteen-five, in an era, as well, when law enforcement was not always approved of in liberal quarters. I came to like my job. The shining badge just like a cop's, the other A.D.A.'s from Saint John's and Fordham with their charcoal suits and political ambitions, the general raffishness, the panorama of New York's streets hauled before me for my judgment. Then too, the fact that Philip started writing Talk of the Town pieces about *me*, "our friend the Assistant D.A." One or two anyway. And all the while I was sensing myself or trying to, keeping words out of my head, looking, listening, in the world but not of it, as was said, as we said. At work it sometimes seemed like a sneaky trick, like fucking in the mop closet.

I played my efficient part revolving the door of Manhattan's justice until nine o'clock and returned to the loft. Maisie and Bobby and Joe were still watching movies. Now it was *Mighty Joe Young*, the old King Kong knockoff, Joe croaking in delight every time the gorilla got a good one in. Half-empty Häagen-Dazs pints sat on the table. Another evening at the loft. Joe and Bobby smoking Newports, though Maisie, after her illness, must have quit, and I didn't smoke. My badge of resistance, my guilty secret, my confession of doubt. Which got me neither the pleasure of the tobacco nor the supposed benefit of a relaxed and measured breath, even while permitting me the opportunity for second-hand smoke enough to last a lifetime. Bobby went to do the dishes from dinner. Joe asked Maisie how she'd been. She talked awhile, about finishing her chemo, the group up in Boston getting ready to buy a farm in Haverill, the apartment of her parents in New York that she'd be staying in while they were out of town. Nothing esoteric, just gossip and talk. I wasn't even sure that Joe knew that I'd known Maisie for years. When Bobby came back to the table he said the garbage disposal was screwed up. Joe grunted. "You drop a fork in it?" "Nothing," Bobby said. "Nothing's in it. I mean, I *know* it's probably jammed." "I dropped a diamond ring in a garbage disposal once," Maisie said, then Joe said, "Why don't you two go fuck?"

I don't know why I should have been so surprised. Maybe I wasn't, really.

Bobby seemed embarrassed. His tongue hung slightly loose in his mouth. He looked at Maisie more as if to apologize than anything. My drunken uncle, sorry. He liked her, of course he liked her.

Maisie looked more curious. Like why had Joe said such a thing? Did she look like she needed a fuck? Did they both?

Or maybe he didn't have any reason at all. We let it drop. No one really answered him. Joe got distracted, or pretended to be distracted, as on screen his namesake beat the ten toughest men on earth, including Primo Carnera, in a tug-of-war. Carnera, the old heavyweight champ, then tried to punch the gorilla in the face. Mighty Joe seemed more perplexed than anything by so puny a gesture, and Joe laughed and the rest of us sort-of laughed.

In a little while Joe wandered off to play with his roses. Playing with them was really what he did, he doted on them as if they were children, clipping them, if the branches were especially long, with his nail clipper, lavishing on them tiny amounts of Miracle Gro. Cultivation as play. Joe never said such words, but it was what I understood by watching him, or from those moments, more frequent in the old apartment on Charles Street than in the loft, when, perhaps on account of the breeze from an open window, the scent of the roses wafted across the rooms, infiltrating our senses, penetrating our brains, an intoxicating fog. Cultivating the human mind as play. The "work" as play. These, too.

I didn't much care for the movie and went home. The next day it was plain that Bobby and Maisie had spent the night together. They showed up together and cooked side-by-side and seemed to know each other's moves. A couple times, as rare as stolen kisses, they smiled at each other. The entire group came to dinner. Thirty of us and Maisie, which as I then supposed made us a little like the first Thanksgiving when all the Pilgrims came, when "nuclear family" was a phrase yet undreamed. We told stories. Joe read the story of the Greek and Chinese artists. My high-class vodka was rather a hit. It may have made Joe drunk enough that he started talking about his father. He said something nice about his father. He talked about his father when his mother died, standing as though the wind had hit him. And when he was done and no one knew what to say, he said, "How do people feel now? What are you sensing?" The question went around the room. Mumbles and pieties. I said it reminded me of a song but I couldn't remember which one, which sounded like a cheat but was exactly true. When it came Maisie's turn, she said, "You're a manipulative shit." "Thank you," Joe said.

The dinner Bobby prepared had enough courses for kings, but nothing about it was more delicious than the fact that he'd been cooking less than a year. And he wasn't afraid to cook with Jello, he found Jello to be a fine ingredient. Black cherry Jello, the best. On that could we not all agree? After dinner, we watched *The Thief of Baghdad*, the previous evening having been but a warm-up. Joe laughed as though he hadn't seen it in years. The little thief and his triumph, flying off on his carpet leaving the world of sighs behind. I, too, at its conclusion, had the urge to have a little fun. And I wasn't alone. I went to pee and felt the toilet door resist, a foot or shoulder against it. I waited, the door opened, and Maisie and Bobby came out together.

On cleanup I pitched in. Nearly everybody did, one of those modest mysteries of communalism among thirty birds who were each supposedly minding their own business. Dishes, floor, sink, stove, carpet. I sensed my arms and legs and looked and listened, either that or I was aware of sensing my arms and legs and looking and listening, either that or I was aware of what I imagined was me sensing my arms and legs and looking and listening. Anyway, I felt I was making up for lost ground, after a lot of not sensing.

CHAPTER 4

A DAY IN THE life, *i.e.* the ins and outs of consciousness also known as the narcoleptic's progress, to wit, wake up, sit up, morning exercise, jump the engine, shut eyes, sense, arms, legs, open eyes, look, listen, shower, back to "sleep," dress, back to "sleep," remember to sense, Pepperidge Farm breakfast, last two Orleans, first two Milanos of new pack, back to "sleep," remember to sense, more "sleep," Broadway, Koreans, dry cleaners, back to "sleep," IRT, more "sleep," remember to sense, back to "sleep," sense, N train, sense, back to "sleep," Appearance Part 5 of Criminal Court in and for the County of New York more or less accidental workplace of more or less accidental pilgrim, back to "sleep," low level sensing, AP-5, more "sleep," Diane, beautiful lush Diane of AP-5, back to "sleep," the violet sheen of her skin, its gleam, the swishing of her legs over her stenography machine, back to "sleep," remember to sense, sense, her almond eyes, her silky hair, black, back to "sleep," sense, back to "sleep," remember to sense, more "sleep," hearing on competency of man to assist in his own defense at trial which if he's incompetent he gets remanded to a mental institution upstate, back to "sleep," low level sensing, remember to sense, the man hearing voices in his head, shrink says he's crazy, I say we all hear voices in our head, shrink says this guy can't tell the difference between the ones that are inside and outside, I say none of us can at the moment we're hearing them, judge thinks *I'm* crazy or at least pain in neck, man remanded to Mid-Hudson for sixty days evaluation, back to "sleep," remember to sense, sense, was Diane impressed by my valiant argument I wonder, "sleep," sense, more "sleep," remember to sense, back to "sleep," "sleep," more cases, more "sleep," whores, back to "sleep," gamblers, back to "sleep," is the judge getting paid off I wonder, "sleep," remember to sense, "sleep," sense, sense, back to "sleep," lunch, back to "sleep," Chinatown, more "sleep," Joe's favorite restaurant shrimp and noodles in curry sauce for a dollar sixty-five, back to "sleep," remember to sense, back to "sleep," low level sensing, back to "sleep," Diane, "sleep," AP-5, more "sleep," clean out clear out calendar, back to "sleep," sense, sense, low level sensing, remember to sense, back to "sleep," judge's Tuesday haircut, back to "sleep," joke with Diane about judge's haircut, back to "sleep," maneuver Diane into judge's chamber, "sleep," remember to sense, shut door somehow, somehow smooch Diane, back to "sleep," up against wall sort of half way against wall, her ass against wall, what if Dan comes in, Dan the court officer, what if, what if, Diane wriggles away, sitcom scene, back to "sleep," judge returns with twelve white hairs left on his head, more "sleep," sense, low level sensing, back to "sleep," AP-5 stands adjourned, thirty-seven cases, twelve plea bargains, fourteen adjournments, four dismissals, two warrants issued for non-appearance, one competency hearing, court officer declares, judge raps gavel, Diane packs up stenography machine, another day another dollar, back to "sleep," remember to sense, sense, back to "sleep," but don't go yet Diane, wait a minute Diane, wait up Diane, why not Diane, come on Diane, walk with Diane, night air, rush hour, "sleep" a little sense a little, Broome Street, Diane, at last her apartment, quickie, good, sense Diane lush Diane, good night Diane, tomorrow Diane, back to "sleep," walk, more "sleep," pride in quickie, back to "sleep," sense, north to loft, "sleep," up elevator, dread, shoes off, remember to sense, sense, sense, sense, sense, sense, back to "sleep," get out book, copy book, one hour copying book, to wit, *Maltese Falcon*, back to "sleep," remember to sense, sense, Joe padding around in his slippers, Big Ronald cutting shelves, atmosphere of Christ the carpenter, more "sleep," write, *i.e.* copy for one hour, as yesterday, as tomorrow, sense, become Hammett, sense my hand that writes Hammett, sense, back to "sleep."

All of this, I suppose, the sense of all my days passing thus, reminded me of nothing so much as a certain John Held woodcut from the twenties that Bobby showed me once, a favorite of his, a map of America marked everywhere, like a ditto machine gone crazy, HOT DOG HOT DOG HOT DOG HOT DOG ORANGE DRINK HOT DOG BOOTLEGGER BOOTLEGGER BOOTLEGGER RUMRUNNER RUMRUNNER RUMRUNNER HOT DOG HOT DOG GAS STATION HOT DOG ORANGE DRINK GAS STATION RUMRUNNER HOT DOG HOT DOG.

Bobby loved rawness. "'Twas Christmas in the Pest House." Another Held, another Bobby favorite. Bobby of the sunny grin, boyish, gentle soul.

And "sleep"? "Sleep" meant not sensing. "Sleep" meant not self-remembering. "Sleep" meant forgetting that one day we die. Passing one's life in sleep. Not knowing one was ever alive. What can be done if you don't even know you're alive?

Or that was the theory anyway or the theory as I understood it. Or what was put out as theory. "Those that have ears to hear . . ." Another phrase.

As for my copying *The Maltese Falcon*, Joe was apprenticing me to Hammett. Again, my understanding only. Nobody ever told me such things, least of all Joe. In one of our first talks I had said to him that I was a writer. For writers he held what seemed a bemused contempt, as if you'd do better to be a carpenter or farmer, not messing around in your own delusions, eager to foist your power-mad schemes on others. The only writers Joe seemed to appreciate were sci-fi guys like Dick or hard-boiled detectives. Those and the old mystics, the stories from Philip's apartment. Thus, Hammett. If I wanted to be a writer, apprentice me to the best, or at least someone worth a few laughs. Or journalism. Somehow, journalism passed Joe's smell test as well. Just the facts, ma'am.

And so I copied *The Maltese Falcon* an hour a day, telling myself that if I were Japanese and wished to be a potter I'd mix clay for years before touching a wheel, if I wished to be a painter I'd clean brushes. I sensed my hand copying each word. I held the pencil with so light a grip that the tips of my fingers felt round and whole. I touched the point of the pencil to the page as if I were landing an airplane on an eggshell. I sensed my hand and looked at the page and listened to the band saw and the fretting in the shop and distant taxis and the still air between, all so that the words, Hammett's words, might not appear as subvocalizations in my head but rather go directly through my hand to the notebook, felt, understood, unshadowed.

It was impossible. My eyes could not apprehend, my hand could not write, without the words sounding-off like muffled echoes, mocking my effort.

Go back. Gently. Sense. The pencil in my hand, each finger swimming in air. The pencil itself leaving its sharpness behind on the paper, a dribble, a stain, life.

Now the pencil grows dull with the losses of its own stuff but at another angle due to the exact same attritions it's become sharp. I turn the pencil. Sense. Listen. My mind my desire in the end not sturdy enough to resist the slyness of the language: I am writing these words, am I not? I am writing these words of the man from Tacoma who was walking down the street on an ordinary day when a beam fell off a building and nearly killed him. The man, I write, then disappeared from Tacoma without a trace, left a wife and happy family behind. Years later, I write, Spade found him in Spokane with new wife and kids. Because, I write, when life ceased to be ordinary and predictable, the man ceased to be ordinary and predictable. When life became steady again, he became steady again. All this I write. Is it really so big a deal that I am not the first to write it? What is writing, after all?

Contentment with small things. I wrote *The Maltese Falcon*. I was an apprentice to greatness.

Though left to my own devices I might have picked Proust. Joe who may never have heard of Proust would, I was quite sure, not have approved. Too fey for a kike from Bensonhurst, too whatever else. *What was this bullshit?*

Go back. Gently. Sense.

I write single-spaced in a composition book. When I fill the composition book I begin another. I am like a medieval scribe.

And when I am done and putting away my composition book, Joe half-waddles by in his corduroy pants and asks if I feel like some chow, he's throwing something in the wok.

Joe's watery eyes, his bulldog frame. As an architect he'd built power plants and sports stadiums. Well, fair enough.

He no longer practiced. He'd quit when he got cancer. Threw it all into the Self, the building and saving of Selves, his own first of all. His teacher some daffy Jew painter, or that was the guy's affect anyway, who painted butterflies and bees and who spoke like South Amboy and had studied with somebody who was somebody and seen Gurdjieff passing through or by.

Though we weren't Gurdjieff people. Or at least Joe never said we were. We had no self-description. Unless we were beggars, mongrels of the spiritual. Gurdjieff-Sufi-Buddhist-Hindu-Jew-New York-mutt the glory the secret sinew of our city.

Sufi mostly? Gurdjieff?

How could I know? Were the two the same?

I loved the poetry. I loved that Joe taught at Pratt now. I loved the power. I loved the straight or crooked line, and that Joe cooked with garlic and meat.

No vegetarian this boy. Yet there was a delicacy to Joe with food. His supple wrist when he flicked the spatula. His fingers, thick and muscular, yet supple; his thumb, gripping the strainer, the peanut oil dribbling down, spattering the wok. Joe cooked with noise, and taught Bobby how to cook with noise.

Dinner on glossed blue Arabia plates on the long particle board table trimmed with cherry. Joe made everything himself, his furniture, his food. Though the loft itself was a work in progress. Ty Duncan had bought it for him, or loaned him the money on negligible terms, part of Ty's winnings when the *Lampoon* went national. We who were as establishment as we were subversive, like a secret cell in an officer corps. Joe had only moved in in September, which

I was sure was part of what the "event" after Christmas was about. Getting the loft into shape, finishing the painting, finishing the ceiling and floors. Cheap labor, so went my line. Though it was Joe's position, one of those "positions" he occasionally took, with volubility and an air of certainty as if you could almost hear the quotation marks, that he had no need for so large a loft and only bought it so that we could work on ourselves and it was slower and more expensive to have us work while sensing than to call in a crew of Puerto Rican painters.

Was Joe a bully? Was Joe insecure?

He turned on the TV. Avoiding all the news, local or national, landing on an old John Wayne picture. Joe styling himself rather after the moguls, of Hollywood not Delhi, films in his vocabulary overleaping even movies and becoming directly, inevitably, "pictures." He'd seen this one before. He'd seen everything before, or everything in Technicolor anyway.

Me doing my silent bit by setting the table putting the utensils out. When I was with Joe it was easy to sense. His voice, his skin, his characteristic clothes, his glance so often averted as if he were afraid it might burn you, all of these seeming to radiate remembrance.

Though if I'd simply seen him in the street, a man hardly tall, minding his own business? It was easy, as well, to fantasize. Joe without doing or saying anything to or about me, just sitting there thick and sturdy shoveling rice and pork into his mouth his bowl up to his lips like a bib, watching an old western, two shoes off his thick feet, his black socks on the table, evoked in me a sense of being small beyond compare, awash in everything I'd ever felt for my father, teachers, big kids, cops, bosses, building inspectors, driving instructors, the famous, the rich, anyone else in whose shadow I ever fell who looked like they could or might cut my balls off. Or forget the balls, forget psychology forget even evolutionary biology. Somewhere in the thick folds of our secrecy we were talking about eternity.

Joe asked if I wanted seconds and helped himself. I had little to say. I took a little more. Words dried up in my throat. I kept waiting for some to appear that I hadn't rehearsed. Only these had a chance, only these were so-called real. The live wire of speech. Had I not a spontaneous bone in my body? I felt embarrassed, poor, without re-source. Joe cackled at something on the screen. I poured the coffee into mugs, poured the half-and-half. No sugar for either of us because that's how Joe liked it. Joe smoked a couple of Newports. I felt embarrassed letting him smoke alone. Would he note my lack of con-viviality? A small personality, one whom the grander gestures escaped.

Being there. The two of us as though watching John Wayne was an interesting thing to do. Though, wasn't it? What was uninter-esting about it? Wasn't it more or less as interesting as anything else on the face of the universe, given all the givens? Some turned loaves into fishes, others turned our perceptions of loaves and fishes. Which miracle was greater, or weren't they just the same? Another Joe line. He had any number of them, and enough of them, at their moment of application, seemed to comfort, cure, salve.

My peripheral vision widened. My resentment of him melted away.

Joe as ample Jewish mother?

As soon as I put any of it into words it was gone.

Meeting at 7:30. I got out and arranged the benches. In came the troops silent and grim. Shoes by the door. Does anybody have anything they want to talk about? Tuesday, the no-work night, the talk-about-stuff night. The night you would almost think it was therapy. But everyone here was here because they were dissatisfied with therapy, or didn't believe in it to start. Therapy was ground transportation; here we would fly. Philip, Bobby, Cal Bittker, Ty, Valerie, myself, Liddie, Big Ronald, a half-dozen other birds, one-half the entire group. And Maisie.

The quiet of the sea before the swells come in. Stingy bastards, hoarding the fragments of our ruined personalities, when there was a whole world that could be talked about. Cigarettes and straightened spines and wiggles on the benches and finally Bobby, about the job he got at *Harper's*, offering it up to Joe like a fatted lamb for acceptance or contempt. Not the job itself but the words, were they real, was there any "I" behind them, or were they all just another part of some endless mechanical program, conditioned, habituated, sleep-walking, sleep-talking? The room placing its bets and waiting, or rather I imagined the room betting and waiting, hushed audience before a curtain, while I myself snuck away, into a rushing tide of subvocalizations having to do with Bobby's article, now it was an article he was writing, he could do anything, this boy, cook, clean, fetch, draw, write articles. The article being about paranoia and cooking, which sounded like a joke but who knew what Bobby would write, it would probably be weird and wonderful.

Without thanking Joe directly, Bobby noted that if Joe hadn't turned him into a cook and general houseboy he could never have sold this article.

Joe nodded in noncommittal fashion, as if stepping gingerly in a field of words that must be booby-trapped, with bits of confession, flattery and gratitude all looking almost alike; but he seemed pleased with his handiwork. "I told you! I told you!"

An appropriate-enough title, I thought. Cooking and Paranoia. Joe had contempt for me—what other conclusion to draw? Why should I alone be starved? Which was to say that Bobby was getting paid for articles when the only thing Joe told me was to quit writing. Not that I wanted to write articles, but wasn't it a start? I sat there, black tar bubbling up in my throat, and would I dare to say what it was while it still tasted fresh and oozy, I who at the moment could recall hardly one thing in my life I'd ever said that was truly dangerous, that I knew in advance would make me sound ridiculous. Blurt out your life, here and now, why not—I managed to think for a moment before the words all but blotted out the thought—what more can you lose, have you not already lost everything? What else could this group be about, if it is not the club of those who lost everything?

Lost everything or gave everything up or was there really any difference?

Bobby talked about the shitty pay he'd be getting from *Harper's* and Joe, who was a practical man as well as an impractical one, counseled him to do a good job this time and make up for it next time which sounded to me fatuous and true at once and Bobby nodded and said, "Right." Bobby and Joe. My despair at perfect marriages. A prayer of the wounded, flushing my face and heating my eyes. I said, without hearing the words until they were in the air, "I'm feeling . . . a little envious."

Joe's watery eyes swept my way, his thick neck like a gun turret. My vision widened, my mouth dried up.

"Oh? Of who?" His voice unexpectedly soft, as if cosseting something precious.

"Bobby," I said, feeling I'd said something right for once, already forming the words of self-congratulation that would send me back to sleep.

"You're envious of *him*? . . . He's envious of *you*?" Joe's delighted whoop. Though who else could I have been meaning, was Joe play-acting or was he dense? "Why are you envious of Jeeves?"

Joe's eyes ticked back and forth between us.

"All the usual suspects, I guess."

"Guess you'll just have to suffer," Joe said, with an offhand fierceness, even glee, to show he was unimpressed. Then, in a more modulated tone, as though he'd just mulled it over and his conclusion was the same, he repeated, "Guess you'll just have to suffer."

Suffering being another one of those things that Joe talked about, but, unlike many others who wrapped themselves around this endlessly fascinating topic, with neither sentimentality nor blame, like a Zen master's stick. "Suffer" meant don't act like a baby and don't waste my time. "Suffer" meant you've got to be kidding. But it also meant, in some deeper register whose resonance I faintly caught, self-remembrance, the only escape, the only honorable way. Joe smothered the ways and means of the everyday world in a relentless, suffocating irony, yet he seemed also to get a nostalgic pleasure from them, in the Japanese fashion, nostalgia for the evanescent.

Was I part of the floating world or a dead weight? Joe's attention snapped back to Bobby. I felt like I'd dared everything for nothing.

"How do you feel? You've got a secret envier."

"Flabbergasted," Bobby said.

"What does that mean?"

"A little bit flabber, a little bit gassed."

While they were talking about something I said, neither was looking my way. I was like the rabbit that got the greyhounds going and then disappeared.

"Where are you right now?" Joe asked him.

"A little bit behind myself," Bobby said. "In the woods."

"Cold and dark in the woods?"

"Yes."

"Try stepping forward. Can you? Can you step forward a couple steps?"

"Yes."

"Did you?"

"Yes."

"Still in the woods?"

"No."

"Catch up with yourself?"

"Yes."

"Any little shadows?"

"Can't see any."

"Feel better?"

"Uh-huh."

"Just stay there then. Just enjoy it for a little while."

Joe's cosseting voice again, wrapping up Bobby like an infant.

I had no idea what they were talking about. I was utterly lost, in whatever woods Joe was referring to or some other woods or in no woods altogether. For a moment my envy, my resentment, my sarcasm, all evaporated, as if in conformity to some newly discovered law of physics purporting to describe envy's inability to survive too great a distance between the envious and envied. Bobby and Joe sat there like two guys on a walkie-talkie in the darkness. The rest of us dead quiet. Fragments of words, half-phrases, kicked around my head like incomplete crosswords. Mostly quiet; fires tamped down. All I felt was the luck of being on a journey to the unknown, even in steerage.

Maisie stifled a giggle.

CHAPTER 5

"WHY DO YOU HAVE to be a *young* writer?" Joe asked me once. "Why can't you be an *old* writer?"

*

Biographical explanations for why they came to the group.

Cal, because his whole life had been money and music, one of those kids from Park Avenue who play Carnegie Hall when they're fifteen and where do you go from that? Because his father, a furrier, the "king of sable," lost all the money one day? Because his music depended entirely on precision, it gloried in its precision, advertised its precision, but one day in secret Cal discovered that nothing in the world was precise?

Liddie, because the Church had disappointed her, she might have been a nun but she liked to fuck? Because for a long time no one wanted to fuck her?

Valerie, because something weird's expected of you when you grow up near that UFO highway in New Mexico and you're cracker-jack smart to boot? Because she slept with Carlos Castenada, more or less at the height of his fame, and realized what a blowhard he was? Because she really, really, really wanted to be the best little girl in the world?

Big Ronald, because you never knew with these Okies, they're slyer than you think? Because, bouncing off a divorce, he liked the anti-family, the loose women, the lack of stupid questions? Because his favorite uncle had been a preacher, and what that had to do with it he wasn't sure, but he thought something, something about love, something about things you don't really talk about, not in Tulsa anyway—and was this a question too?

Philip, because his father was a communist or accused of being a communist and it was all sort of an embarrassment and an incon-venience and a blotch on the family escutcheon and it made child-hood hard and confusing and what could be more opposite to being a communist but at the same time sort of the same (in its social as-pects, its *cogniscenti* aspects) than this? Because he had a tender, spiritual nature that hoped for the best for the world? Because he had all this anger bottled up, and after shrinks and liberal Episcopal bishops and drugs and repressed sex and sitting in his bathtub many, many hours he still had it?

Ty, because he won the lottery with the *Lampoon* and he wasn't the type to splurge? Or because he was precisely the type to splurge, to bet it all, to believe in nothing or all of it? Because the inside of his mind, as he once described it, tasted as dry as the stuff inside a pencil sharpener, and he was desperate for a cool drink? Because the professional cynic with his chewed-up pipe stem, more than most, needs something?

Maisie, because she'd gone through too many shrinks and they'd all more or less fallen in love with her—with her or her money or family—so she didn't trust them anymore? Because of McLean's? Because of Hodgkin's?

Bobby, because he came from Shaker Heights which was almost like coming from Great Neck and if you were from Shaker Heights and were a light spirit afoot in the world you were supposed to do something about it, make your statement, make your escape, fly away? Because when he was seven years old his mother lay on the chaise by the pool and loosened her swimsuit strap and had Bobby slather her back with suntan lotion?

I could go on. There were thirty of us, after all. Thirty-one, including Maisie. Or also we could take a closer look, zoom in, more a shrink's-eye view, Maisie's this-and-that, Bobby's this-and-that, Philip's this-and-that.

Would it help? Would it explain?

For a long time, biographies seemed like lies, stories we told ourselves to avoid the fact that when it came to what we were doing, we all had the same story.

We were here. We had got here. Where did we go from here?

*

At a meeting once I tried to explain why I had begun to write. I said it was because it beat getting a job, but that didn't sound right. I said it was to be the best, because I had to be the best, but that didn't sound right. I said because you could live and explain life to yourself as you went, you could chew it all, the flavor would last longer, it wouldn't be over so soon, but that didn't sound right. I said it was to be famous and get girls, but that didn't sound right. I said it was for immortality, but that didn't sound right. I said maybe it was just because I liked the sounds of words, I liked hearing them in my head, phrases, little speeches, they reassured me somehow, comforted me, made me feel brave in a weird way, I didn't know who else could have so many words in their head, crowded in there, packed, chockablock, and wasn't that a sign? But that didn't sound right, and I said so. I said none of them sounded right. My voice was gruff.

"Why are you telling me this?" Joe asked.

"I don't know. I'm not sure."

"Are you writing now?"

"Just the hour a day, copying."

"What are you tasting now?"

"My saliva. It's sweet."

"Do you hate me for taking your misery away?"

"Yes. I do."

*

Bobby: wren.

Philip: robin.

Cal: hawk.

Valerie: crow.

Ty: scarlet tanager.

Liddie: flamingo.

Big Ronald: mockingbird.

Maisie: oriole.

*

A list I wrote once. Are the birds less than rare, the choices a bit obvious? As little as I knew about people, I knew less about birds. My friends: was I right even one time?

*

Joe, on one occasion, on the value of the "work."

"I can't tell you what it is. If I could tell you, I would. But nobody can do that for someone else. You have to find it for yourselves.

"What value does it have for *you*? Really, you should be asking yourselves that.

"If it doesn't have any value for you, why be here? Aren't there pleasanter things you could be doing?"

CHAPTER 6

THE *BIRD GUIDE*. ALMOST on the periphery, yet a full picture of whatever it is I'm picturing (or *us*; is it *us*?) cannot be had without it. The *Bird Guide*, our magazine. Or really, it was Philip's magazine, and Cal's, and Bobby's, and after I was around for awhile, a little bit mine. We published it twice a year with a black-and-white cover out of Philip's narrow *New Yorker* office, where boxes of old copies were stacked up along with old railroad timetables and leads for "Talk of the Town" stories. It cost sixty-five cents, or as was said from the first issue, "still only sixty-five cents." Inflationary times. Its subscribers included the *New Yorker*'s editor Shawn, most of Cal Bittker's East Side relatives, Andy Warhol, a few public libraries, some publishing types, the New York City Police Department's Public Information Office, and a miscellany of wise souls and oddballs who saw it at the half-dozen newsstands where we managed to display it, the 72nd Street IRT subway station, the bookstore on Spring Street, the Gotham, and the one on Eighth

Street. "The best zip codes in the business," total circulation four hundred fifty.

You could call it a cult magazine, but we never did. It already existed when I first went to Philip's apartment, and it was funnier then than it was later. It published Bobby's explosive cartoons featuring Mister All-Electric Kitchen and others, snippets of the Sufi stories that were read at Philip's on Thursday evenings, musical scores by Cal and his composer pals, various articles that Shawn had commissioned for the *New Yorker* but subsequently found too bloody or flaky, pieces by non-professional writers about things they had a peculiar passion for, famously bad cars or gardening in the Shetland Islands *circa* 1935, and police photos. When Joe came along, in my view, the *Bird Guide* started downhill. As Philip grew more serious about the group, the magazine lost some of its cockeyed irony. We published more articles that seemed to have a point, even some with a self-helpy flavor. I felt like I'd been born after the Golden Age. Though not entirely—and this I attributed to Joe seldom paying the magazine much mind. We still published such esoterica as the classification of male and female sexual organs in the work of Sir Richard Burton (the "crowbar," the "importunate," the "vast one") and reviews of Memphis barbecue joints written by a famous pornographer while he was on trial there for obscenity.

On the evening of the *New Yorker*'s 1978 Christmas party, we were moving the *Bird Guide* out of Philip's office and into our new, plainly more ample quarters in Joe's loft. I had regrets about moving at all. Like a rebellious girl from a good family, part of the *Bird Guide*'s seduction of me was how comfortably it still rested in the *New Yorker*'s staid old bosom. We were the anti-*New Yorker*, the camp-following devourer of its rejects, the little engine that could when the great big one couldn't or wouldn't. But would we still be any of those things once we were gone from the eighteenth floor? The lore of the *New Yorker*'s offices, the eighteenth floor, the nineteenth floor, the faded paint and file cabinets everywhere and old maps on the wall, the utter lack of a decorator's hand, the aura of a place where things had been piling up for fifty years and no one spoke much above Shawn's whisper—mere contiguity to these left me with a feeling of being somehow part of a world, the way copying Hammett everyday made me feel somehow tough and writerly. Maybe the janitors felt the same. Even the surly girl at the eighteenth floor reception who grudgingly buzzed us in was writing a novel as she sat there. Did she too feel that she was *New Yorker* material, and if she wasn't was it only because she was too good for it? Were we interlopers in her eyes, competition? With a chip on a shy shoulder, I sat on the gritty old Khorassan in Philip's office emptying the contents of the *Bird Guide*'s file cabinet into boxes, a melancholy exercise, not least because three or four boxes would hold all there was of it. Bobby sorted out expired subscriptions. Philip was off making the punch for the Christmas party, a duty which might have fallen on him or which he could conceivably have sought; he said he was mixing up a doozy. It being his feeling, generally speaking, that the *New Yorker* staff was a decent bunch but unwholesomely reserved such that an overdose of alcohol once a year could be hoped to be more tonic than fatal. A Fishhouse punch, all rum and vodka and a touch of sherbet to hide the implications, once concocted at the Union League in Philadelphia or someplace like that. Philip had ancestors who ran in such circles, before the later generations turned lefty. I was feeling, too, a little like Cinderella uninvited to the ball— or worse, missing her last fucking chance for the ball since next year we'd be downtown in our new digs—when Philip, turned out like some Ivy League P.T. Barnum with a carnation in his blazer, poked his head in to say we could come to the party if we wanted, if it wouldn't be too boring, Renata Adler'd brought three or four Belgians so if there were Belgians why not us.

In the corridor Philip was ladling out the punch and Bobby knew all the cartoonists, leaving me to my own devices. There were maybe fifty people mingling around in shirtsleeves, workshirts, the occasional old J. Press tweed, plastic cups were piling up on the file cabinets. I sipped my Fishhouse punch like all the rest and realized that the din was gaining. I struggled to keep my bearings. People looked at me as though wondering who I was and how I got there. I had the right clothes but the wrong face. I felt a certain melancholy resignation that an opportunity, once cherished, was slipping away. Could I not speak to someone, say one thing? It was I who was sensing myself, after all, I who was leading a secret life stiffened with peculiar insight and hope that these ordinary souls had no clue of, it was I who was rich in my poverty, so why was I still so scared? Even to tell them I was an Assistant D.A. And not any Assistant D.A., but *our friend* the Assistant D.A. The more I sipped my second glass of punch, the more my worlds seemed to collide. Which one was the dream? I would probably have left without a word to a soul if Bobby hadn't pushed by and introduced me to a cartoonist pal of his, a sweet-seeming man half as woolly as his characters who in the accelerating turnover, propelled by the punch, in turn introduced me to a film critic with mousy hair and librarian glasses whose reviews were celebrated at the time. She too had been drinking the punch. So had everybody. The room was getting loud.

I told her I was a friend of Philip's.

Philip would have a lot to answer for in the morning, she said agreeably enough.

I said I worked on the *Bird Guide,* and did she know what that was?

"Of course I know."

"But you don't subscribe."

"No."

"Would you like to subscribe?"

"Actually, no. Why would I want to subscribe? I don't understand what it's about."

She seemed annoyed by the whole subject, as though it had been an irritant for some time.

"Do things you don't understand irritate you?" I asked.

"Well what's the point, really? Really, what's the point?"

"Would you like me to show you the point?"

"It's all so shapeless. Maybe *that's* the problem, it's shapeless. It doesn't have a shape."

"Do you think the world has a shape?"

"Maybe not. But magazines should. All the more so if the world doesn't."

"Why don't we go to Philip's office and I'll get out a copy and I'll show you the point," I said.

"It's the shape," she said.

"Oh, so now it's the shape."

"It has no shape."

"Then let's go to Philip's office and I'll show you the shape."

And so we went to Philip's office. She continued to sip from her plastic cup and to complain about Philip's malicious punch. What's happened to him, she wanted to know, he's gone off some deep end.

"Bad company," I said.

"I didn't mean you. I wasn't accusing you."

"And I'm not accusing you," I said.

I showed her the *Bird Guide* that was mostly about smoking. "This is our smoking issue," I said.

I laid out the magazine on Philip's oak desk, pulled the chain on his banker's light and showed the pages under its yellow-green glare.

"You see, it's in favor of smoking. It says smoking's good for you."

"But that's ridiculous, it isn't," she said.

"But neither's that harsh, puritanical, self-righteous put-down of smokers that everybody's into now. It's just a way of people scoring points on others, it's hatred, it's aggression."

"You're telling people to go kill themselves!"

"We're just telling people to relax, life's not as bad as it seems. Unless, of course, it's worse."

"I've been trying to quit for three years."

"I don't smoke myself."

"There's no point to this."

"But at least there's a shape. You can see the shape, at least."

"What's the point?"

"I can't say."

"Well if *you* can't even say . . ."

"I thought we were talking about shape."

"*And* points."

"I can show you. Here it is."

"What's *this*? What's *this*?"

She was looking at another article now.

"*Labial beauty?*"

"Some people are interested in that."

"So what? So *what*? It's not even obscene. At least if it were obscene . . ."

"I'm not defending every article. But you can see the point."

"It's *stupid*."

"It is. Agreed."

"Well then . . ."

"If you're so stupid that you think nothing in the world's ever allowed to be stupid"—I said—"or at least not in your hallowed corridors, nothing stupid allowed on the eighteenth floor . . . You're narrow-minded, Miss _____. There's no room for stupidity in your universe, when in fact in the real world stupidity's all over the place. We of the *Bird Guide* are getting a handle on it at least."

"I'm certainly not narrow-minded."

"You are so narrow-minded that you know what? We're sick of your condescending patronizing glances every time you walk by our door—we're moving out of here! We're moving to freer territory."

"I didn't say you should do that."

"What do you think all these boxes are about?"

"So you were moving out *already!*"

"And you know what else, you know what else, you're so narrow-minded? I was going to let you give me a blow job but now I'm not."

"I think I want to get more punch," she said.

"I realize I may have blown my chance to send you my movie reviews," I said as she stepped out the door, "but my cock says no and I back it up!"

So much for networking, which may, by the way, have been a new word that year. So much, as well, for *bien pensant*'s take on the *Bird Guide*, and by extension, for sure, our little rogue band.

Better to keep your mouth shut.

But why?

It wasn't so bad, to be a scoundrel, to feel so young, I who had never really felt young even when I was.

To whom does the future belong, after all?

In the world but not of it. Give them a taste of this or that.

I felt for a moment like a man who'd cut off the bridge he was standing on.

And was I proud of it, yes or no?

Stop. Go back. Gently. Sense yourself. Are you there at all?

Later we went downtown in a cab together, Philip and Bobby and I. Nobody said anything.

In the meeting it was Philip who spoke. I tried to sense while the room whirled away, but it was his voice alone that steadied me. Philip was the only one of us who when he had something to say in a meeting spoke in an entirely conversational tone, as though really speaking to a friend.

But weren't we all friends? Wasn't even Joe a friend?

Who is your friend if it's not one who helps you?

Go back. Don't speculate. Don't say to yourself "speculate." Sense.

The room steadied. Philip's voice, slightly reedy, flat, the cadences of his sentences like the lengths of an easy breath. "I'd say the party went well until the third punch bowl."

"Oh, how *was* the punch?" Joe asked.

"Effective. And tasty."

"Shawn there?"

"Nah. He hates parties. Or at least big parties, where he could forget somebody's name. But Galen Townsend was there."

"Oh?"

"Somebody's guest."

"And?"

"And nothing. . . . Nothing, really. We said hello . . . perfectly cordial."

When Joe wished to keep a conversation floating, he lit a cigarette. The rituals of a new package. The crinkling of the cellophane.

Then, in a slightly lower register, as though abruptly the thera-
pist, vocal downshifting, asking Philip to dig deep: "What did you
feel?"

"Nothing. Really. Nothing."

"I'll never sleep with you," Joe said.

"Good."

Philip said this a little bravely, added, "I never thought you
would."

I was certain Joe would then say: you never even imagined it?
But he didn't. He let it drop.

I should put in here that it had never occurred to me that Philip
was queer. Nor was the group exactly a queer-friendly place. The
subject would come up from time to time and we attracted our share,
but Joe mostly seemed to view homosexuality as a distraction from
the work, or perhaps a disability as well, in the same way that being
a writer or drug-taker, even of pot, was a disability. Carpenters were
good for the work. Normal people, normal habits, were good for the
work. Complications, twists, special pleadings, were just a pain in
the ass. Joe viewed everything, mercilessly, in terms of its usefulness
to what we were doing. In furtherance of which, he'd made a match
between Philip and Liddie, the F-train girl and the Talk of the Town
guy, part of his plan to "normalize" Philip, which involved, as well,
the substitution of Philip's old pink plastic prep school glasses with
aviator frames, the growth of a mustache and sideburns, and some
serious weight gain, with the result that Philip looked less like a
grown-up altar boy and more like a seventies incarnation of Teddy
Roosevelt as police commissioner. In truth, I preferred the old Philip
to the makeover, but Philip himself plainly went for the "new guy."

If anyone from the group's early members was a true believer, it was he, or at least he cut Joe the most slack, was most resourceful in defending him against perceived slights, and seemed on the surface, anyway, the most transformed of anybody. His old writer's block was gone, he was banging out Talk stories, he no longer did drugs or spent whole mornings in the bathtub.

After the meeting, Philip, Bobby and I walked up Broadway together. A little December night air to sober up, and anyway I was feeling comradely. Though I might mention here the unspoken hierarchy that made us something other than three cheerful musketeers, and that overlay even the fact that Bobby was the group mascot and everyone loved Bobby. If somebody had diagrammed us as a corporate power chart, Joe would of course have stood at the top, with Philip his first lieutenant and Bobby under Philip and myself under Bobby, exactly in the order we'd been introduced to Joe, and with other shoots of authority stemming from Liddie, who was from "the old group." Or to put it another way: if we imagined ourselves in an esoteric group with secrets to be transmitted, these might be expected to run from Joe through Philip to Bobby then me, or to Liddie directly. Although, as was often said and was actually inscribed in the spare, wistful watercolor which I imagined was a gift from Joe's old teacher that hung on the wall in back of Joe's Eames chair, "Sometimes those that are near are far and sometimes those that are far are near."

The fact that Philip looked after Bobby and Bobby looked after me diminished not at all the admiration I felt for Philip. It equaled the fondness I felt for Bobby and far exceeded anything I felt for Joe. My problem with Joe was first that he didn't care enough for me and second his frightening, destructive vulgarity, his raw power, that had turned the heads of Philip and Bobby and converted Philip's sedate little reading group into a world-defying adventure. Or you could also say that this was Joe's allure, even to me. But getting back to Philip, whom I could love (though love was a word in dispute in the group, not that it was but what it was, Joe insisting that love could only be an action, compounded of kindness, attention and respect, or anyway that its existence could only be proved by such an action, and that the puny or morbid feelings that people usually plastered with love's label were nothing more than conditioning, habit, confusion, pathology which might or might not accompany the real thing but most often stood fatefully in the way of it) without fear. Philip was first off the finest writer I knew and yet he wrote about nothing but New York. His love stories, his historical epics, his lyric bouts with nature, were all compressed into prosy eight hundred word blocks about butcher shops and circuses and new restaurants and street fairs and the theater with the most flops on Broadway. His sentences ran like babbling brooks, running over rocks, hitting surprises, gurgling, picking up nouns, turning onto fresh vistas, ending who knew where, with some lonely first person plural somewhere looking on as in a Hudson River painting with a train, giving the whole its human dimension, its hope, its nostalgia, its curiosity. For a long time I wondered how Philip had come to know and love the city so well. He'd grown up in Berkeley and gone to Harvard from there and hadn't come to New York and the *New Yorker* until graduating from the *Crimson*. But it turned out there was a lacuna in his life. His father had been in the Berkeley physics department, a friend of Oppenheimer's, blacklisted in the fifties and fleeing to Mexico at the same time that Philip's mother had a nervous breakdown. So for three years in the fifties they'd shipped him off to friends in New York, rich Jews, old family of East Side liberals, who'd introduced him, with grace and openhandedness, to a charmed East 82nd Street life. The result being that Philip became a poet not of seventies New York but of an older, more refined, and maybe grayer thing, something like what Woody Allen aimed for in *Manhattan*, though Allen himself was a creature of New York in the seventies, singles bars on Second Avenue and cute meets in Laundromats. These things were not omitted from Philip's New York, but they didn't hold pride of place. That went to the old restaurants whose eulogies he wrote, the side street second floor restaurants, the bus routes, the toy train shops on 45th Street, the remnants of the El's, the steam heat in rent-controlled buildings, and how it all got there.

We stopped on Eighth Street for takeout coffee, and when we got to Sixth Avenue Bobby kept going west. Philip and I walked north and for the first time since the meeting I remembered, as if it were something that if I paid it little enough attention, like a canker sore or a headache, might just go away, something about Philip being queer. What was it exactly that Joe said? *I'll never sleep with you?* And who was Galen Townsend? None of it, through the gauze of detachment I half-consciously tossed over it, made too much sense and in any event he was fucking Liddie now. And who cared anyway where penises were put? We had enough else to be concerned with. Mine had been in enough sleazy places.

But still. Go back. Gently. Sense. Walking side-by-side past Balducci's with my friend. The avenue all but deserted, its sidewalks anyway which were the things that in Philip's New York counted, a breeze out of the west. Walking with Philip, I felt not so much that I owned the city as that I didn't care who owned it.

Go back. Gently sense. Listen to the breeze.

"Who was Galen Townsend?" I asked.

"Oh. He was my boyfriend. Back in college."

"You had a boyfriend in college?"

"Of course." And a few steps later: "Just one more Harvard fairy."

Go back. Sense. Listen.

Would I ever say to Philip I'll never fuck you, would he ever say that to me, no of course not I don't think so but it would never happen anyway not in my lifetime not in many, of that you can be assured, of that I could be assured.

Friends walking along; Twelfth Street. Avoiding the dogshit where the sidewalk narrowed for the boxed-in trees and the garbage bags and then a gypsy cab that had been crawling down the block pulled up beside us and a black guy got out.

A smooth brown leather jacket, belted, a beard, a big guy. I thought he wanted directions.

"Are you Diane's friend?" he asked.

"Who? Diane Leeson?"

"Don't be an asshole," he said, and he started to thump me.

He was a big guy but he could have been a small guy and still killed me.

I fell to the sidewalk and hoped it wasn't in shit and he kicked me as I curled up. "Smartass! Smartass!"

It's about all he said, asshole and smartass.

I tried to sense myself as the toe of his boot found my groin and this worked in an unanticipated way, turning everything into sensation, undifferentiating the pain. For once I felt sensing myself had some immediate usefulness.

And then I saw Philip, a hapless, fallen expression on his face, as though all of this was beyond him. He shouted help and called for a cop but there wasn't a cop around and he pulled at the guy's arms but the guy at once yanked free of him, as readily as a circus strongman might pull away from the kitschy blandishments of a clown.

I saw Philip's calm rabbit eyes in the middle of his face's commotion and I was embarrassed for him, as I might have been if he was my father and if it was he, my father and not me, who was abjectly losing this fight.

As well, I saw his sideburns and cop's mustache for a moment as but a mask, tokens of an earnest enough aspiration, betrayed.

The guy rolled me over with his foot and kicked my ass and then less sportingly the back of my head and the miracle was—I sensed this miracle—that I still wasn't thinking of myself.

I caught Philip's expression again, rueful more than anything, his fear fading into something more resigned, at the moment he launched his coffee underhanded at the big guy's face.

The guy yipped like a bitten dog, swiped at his nose and cheeks with the back of his hand, but whether the coffee hurt him or was more like a wake-up call to remind him to get the hell out of here before someone in the brownstones called 911 I couldn't be sure. But he backed off, went back to the cab. Unafraid to show his face, which was a little bit bony and bearded, pockmarked with eyes like coals under heavy brows.

He must have known I'd never prosecute; even, that I had the power to call the cops off. He must have known, as well, not to hurt me badly.

Off went the gypsy cab, dragging its tailpipe banging and sparking down the potholed block like a cat with a can on its tail, in only a slightly greater hurry than on its arrival.

Saint Vincent's was only a block away. Philip lifted me up and cleaned my face of mucus and blood with the handkerchief from his blazer and when no cab came walked me slowly, like a patient a day after surgery on his first tour of the hospital sunroom, towards the Saint Vincent emergency.

I thanked him for throwing the coffee.

The least I could do, Philip said.

I explained to him why I could never prosecute, while privately reviewing whether continuing to feel up Diane in the judge's chambers was really such a wise idea.

Then, back to sensing, looking and listening. For the moment there was plenty to sense.

The place was busy for a Tuesday night. I heard a nurse say that anyway. People lined up in rows of plastic chairs like it was an unemployment office. The sicker or more assertive of us spread out over two or three seats, or rested a head on a lover's lap. One guy with a stab wound was bold enough to take occupancy of an empty gurney, but the nurse chased him off. His stab wound was pretty minor. Fluorescent lights shone down on us all like a chilly benediction.

Philip phoned Bobby, who came over with more coffee. I was going nowhere fast. The bruises on my face were complaining more angrily and something in my abdomen ached. But nothing seemed to be broken, no bones anyway.

An hour passed, then an hour-and-a-half. Bobby maliciously sketched the nurses and doctors, filling every unprinted-upon inch of the bag from the coffee shop and the napkins he found inside it. This was probably to cheer me up but could also have been to cheer himself up. I laughed a little at the cartoons but was otherwise bored. We all were. I kept telling my friends to go home. At two o'clock Bobby did. There were still at least fifteen people ahead of me. Philip fell asleep with his arms folded, like a Buddha who'd chosen to die, and I dozed off as well. I had a dream that we were in a church under attack somewhere in Europe, for some reason I thought Barcelona, or Bordeaux, and guys with black helmets and faces like rusted iron were finding us, finding Philip and me, who ran out of the church but were paralyzed as we ran, turned into pillars of salt as the rusted iron guys launched their napalm from their guns and my face screamed in the blinding white blast of wind that overtook us. I woke up with the bruises under my eyes burning and my cut lip miserably swollen. Philip got me a couple of Tylenols from the nurse but it was still going to be an hour. I felt Philip's soft concern. It would probably be an hour and a half. Philip struck up a conversation with the guy in the chair on the other side of him, a slight, dark-skinned guy in a beret. The guy's voice sounded like "the islands," even if I couldn't place which island, or at the moment exactly where any of "the islands" were. It turned out he was from Brazil and they talked about Pelé for awhile and then the guy, who said he himself was feeling malarial but it was no big deal, asked what was wrong with me.

Stupid question, he then concluded, on looking at my face. But he was rather quick to understand that this must have something to do with a woman.

Philip complained to him about the wait, or rather complained and simultaneously explained, because this guy was from São Paulo and might not know that New York was broke.

The guy said in São Paulo this was nothing, the clinic took all day.

I suggested to Philip we fuck it and leave.

"But why? I help you," the guy from São Paulo said.

It was Philip, not I, who asked him, "How?"

The guy raised his hands, showed his outstretched fingers, like a mime. "If he lets me." He looked at me benignly enough, as if he could understand my skepticism.

However doubtful I was, Philip was less so. Or maybe he just wanted to go home so anything was worth a try.

"Sure. Okay," I said, figuring if I said no thanks I'd sound like a prig, more to Philip than the guy.

Philip stood up and so did the guy from São Paulo so that I could stretch across the three plastic chairs with my face up and I sensed myself like crazy as though that would somehow make me a cooperating partner, a conscious man is a healing man, and the man put his thumbs that looked rough but were soft into my wounds in such a way that I feared infection but also felt their probing care.

Or in truth I didn't know what he was doing. I did, however, believe that in certain cases and with certain gifts or practices that spirits could trump bodies.

I believed this because I had to, because if I didn't what was I doing with my life?

The guy's eyes peered down at me on my makeshift operating table as if I were a meal he was preparing and Philip's eyes somehow looked the same, the eyes of cooks or maybe naturalists, and I remembered or thought I remembered that both of them were queer.

I felt, actually, in good hands. When the guy was done my face tingled as though I'd put an astringent aftershave on it but there was little pain. Disproving the notion of time's arrow, I was told I still had an hour or more to wait to see a doctor, even a nurse. I thanked my benefactor and we left. On the same paper that Bobby had sketched the emergency room personnel, Philip took his name and number, because the guy felt a story about himself—it turned out he came into Saint Vincent's nearly every week and laid hands on whoever would let him—might help his immigration status.

We picked up a few bandages at a late-night pharmacy on Seventh Avenue and Philip flagged me a cab. It was almost four o'clock.

And what would I tell my co-workers tomorrow? Maybe I'd skip it, declare a day of world forgiveness.

Philip craned his neck avuncularly through the cab's rear window, as if I were a drunk or an out-of-towner about whom it would be best to remind the driver that he had a lot of local friends. Was there maybe a story in this South American guy, sort of the angel of Saint Vincent's, he asked.

Before in my woozy condition I could make a judgment on this, Philip added as if in afterthought: "Would you like to write it with me?"

"Sure."

"Then okay, we'll do that," he said, "why not."

The "why not" more like punctuation than interrogatory, the way Joe so often said it.

Philip's head, leaning into my cab, at that moment reminded me of a giraffe's in a zoo, benign and herbivorous, leaning over its bars for a peanut.

On the way uptown I wondered if I might have been more effusive in my response to him, more gracious. I decided not. Philip, I decided, was practicing kindness. I was practicing truth. The truth was that I was flattered and a little bit thrilled, but the truth was also that I could see that I was thrilled and I wondered why and this wondering was sobering. What difference did any of it make? Why was I still such a slave? Words in my head, but I listened to them.

CHAPTER 7

A FEW OF THE secrets of us.

A lamp in a niche.

Chakras, yes, more or less, chakras seen through a western eye.

Sex.

Gurdjieff's intervals, Gurdjieff's octaves.

Which is to say the world and all worlds run in octaves, with intervals where the F flats and B sharps ought to be that seem to throw everything off.

Much Gurdjieff detail that seemed cockamamie and as if out of some nineteenth-century sci-fi novel about shooting for the moon and that I never understood but if it mattered, I felt, if Joe really believed this stuff, we were all in bad shape. But I didn't believe he did.

Sex.

To break free, first of all, you must break free of your parents.

We are all of us born alive up shit's creek without a paddle, or in alternative formulation also using the well-regarded article, up to our eyebrows in it.

All religions have their inner truths, and all these inner truths are the same.

People should have an aim.

Self-understanding is all.

But what is a "Self"?

What is an "I"?

We swim in a sea of air.

Breathing is all.

Lots of things are all.

Consistency as the celebrated hobgoblin of the second-rate mind.

What's wrong with a second-rate mind?

Ch'i: breath; but also, spirit.

The sermon on the mount.

Just another kike from Brooklyn.

A little Chinese mud man, lost in mountains.

Lazy. Good. Sweet.

Godzilla.

Errol Flynn.

Hot fudge sundaes.

Japanese transformers.

Vegetarianism is not all, nor is physical fitness.

Cheers for stomachs, for bellies, for good food and glowing coals.

An example of an aim, that you might write on a slip of paper and put in your wallet between your social security card and your cash machine card: always to remember that you're going to die.

Politics are irrelevant, or anyway leave public debate to those who care about it.

Leave the maintenance of the machine to those who care about it.

There will always be people who care about these, and while the world chugs on, others may slip away.

Don't gossip.

Don't argue.

If you want to understand people, mirror them.

Don't attack unless attacked.

Help others.

In whatever ways they can be helped, help them, but what is help when the ship is sinking?

The "work" may or may not be the "path."

Whatever is said about the work is only true or not true, helpful or not helpful, harmful or not harmful, depending on who says it and to whom and when and how and why.

Seek knowledge, even in China.

But it's not necessary to go to India.

In fact, it's better not to. India is vacation, India is running away.

All knowledge must be adapted to the local culture, or imagination enters.

You can't learn except from one who knows.

But if someone's a step above on the ladder, they have that much they can teach you.

To rise on the ladder you have to place someone else on your rung.

All of this is bullshit.

Philip K. Dick is "not bad," Errol Flynn is "not bad," Fred Astaire is "not bad," Sabu is "not bad," King Kong is "not bad."

"Not bad" is about as good as it gets.

You need a group to get anywhere.

Without a group to wake you up you'll fall back asleep.

Without a group you could go crazy.

Even with a group you might go crazy.

You don't have to go to Harvard.

But you need a little meanness, a little ruthlessness, and going to Harvard's proof you've got it.

The elusive "I."

The habitual, false I.

The habitual false I that one moment thinks and likes this and the next moment thinks and likes the other, that is a multiplicity of I's, very nearly infinite I's, all thinking they're the one.

Everyone wants approval all the time for everything.

Be aware of your facial muscles.

Relax your facial muscles.

Be aware of relaxing your facial muscles.

Be aware of all your muscles, be aware of relaxing all your muscles, be aware of not relaxing all your muscles.

Be aware of wanting approval all the time for everything.

Be aware of everything.

Don't change anything, just sense look and listen.

But doesn't that change everything?

Doesn't that make it possible to change everything?

Or even one little thing?

If one little thing is changed, is not everything changed?

Be greedy.

Don't be greedy.

Wake up buddy it's the real world.

It's possible to have something like an orgasm all the time.

A girl looks into a pool and sees the reflection of her lost necklace on a branch just above her head.

If something comes up, follow it.

Don't put others in double binds.

Don't project feelings about your parents onto others.

The world is our oyster.

The banality of writing any of this down.

How if said and heard in person between willing souls the same words that sound so trite on paper might touch the heart or mind, might awaken nobility, love or truth, the real things not kitsch, might stimulate self-remembrance.

Nothing is as it seems on paper.

If you can't get rid of the words in your head try counting from one to one hundred then back down to two, then up to ninety-nine then back to three then up to ninety-eight and down to four and so on up and down and back and forth constantly in your head for a month.

Become like a mirror to the world.

Li Po.

Tu Fu.

Lao Tzu.

Peking duck.

There are no secrets.

Those that have eyes to see and ears to hear.

Old stuff new stuff all the same stuff.

The secrets of pre-sand Egypt.

Freud.

What about him?

Onto something but didn't go all the way.

Transference.

The right use of sex energy.

Is what exactly?

The production of fine energies through conscious effort and attention.

Worlds within worlds.

Movies with instructional value *The Thief of Baghdad*, *The Razor's Edge*, *Kim*, *The Incredible Voyage*, *Willie Wonka and the Chocolate Factory*.

Dikr.

Aladdin's lamp.

Damn the torpedoes! Full speed ahead!

The orgasm inside your head.

Every religion has an outer shell of the faithful and an inner kernel of the knowing.

Life itself is the miracle, rendering other miracles showy and banal.

The Sufi's patched coat.

The Monkey King, the chattering mind.

Secrets best passed in riddles and tales.

*

Biographical explanations for why they came to the group, continued. Example number eight: me.

Because I was lonely in my room. Because I knew I could never write myself out of where I found myself. Because my father left my mother and my world was fractured. Because I became a man too soon. Because my cock told me to. Because I'd go far to get close to the *New Yorker*. Because I'd gone to Brooklyn some months before going to Philip's and had seen at the Brooklyn Academy a performance by Peter Brooke's troupe of "The Parliament of the Birds," performed for free on a Persian carpet laid over a basketball court mostly for kids from Bed-Stuy bused in for the show, and this performance, at once poetic and raw, pitched to the street jocularity of the kids, made an impression of prophecy on me which when I went to Philip's apartment, and then Joe's, seemed somehow confirmed. Because I was a dissatisfied Jew. Because I was broke. Because the long time I spent as interlocutor betwen my father's indifferent cruelty and my mother's hurt rage exhausted me psychically and I was ready for anything. Because it was the seventies. Because it was New York and I was looking like everybody else for the next new thing. Because there'd been too little love in my life. Because I was looking for my father. Because it would give me something someday to write about. Because God was dead.

All I can say, really, is maybe.

CHAPTER 8

NOBODY AROUND THE COURTHOUSE said anything about my pounded face. The stale air of business as usual, as if the fluorescent lights never went out, no domestic beef jokes, no wry comments about the perils of law enforcement. This was after I skipped a day. Now it was Thursday. My bruises may have failed to stand out against the local backdrop.

Or was it another glorious example of conscious healing, your alternative medicine dollars hard at work?

Diane noticed. But I didn't see her till mid-morning because she'd been assigned another courtroom for the day. She was wearing a dress of mauve angora, as if very possibly the entire flotsam of 100 Centre Street had gotten together to crown her their queen. I informed her that due to health considerations and also out of remorse for potentially compromising her professional status through my persistent and inappropriate gestures of affection in potentially revealing and quasi-public circumstances, I would be quitting the more intimate aspects of our acquaintance as of immediately. In words more or less, the way words of disengagement are always more or less. She said she knew who did this to me and he was an asshole and she was sorry. I said thanks, and we were both very cool. All of this *sotto voce* in the din of the fourth floor corridor in the middle of mamas making bail for their boys and lawyers hustling pimps and vice versa, as if we, or particularly I, were part of the human comedy after all.

But where did it all lead?

Sense look and so on be absorbed in this great consciousness all around you be a speck in the universal wonder just don't get too fancy about it. Nor too fancy about not getting too fancy, nor too plain about it, nor too plain about being plain, nor too prideful nor too critical or nothing at all. One's mind can spin like a top. One's mind can do a dervish dance all by itself. As consciously as I could I silently wished for Diane success in all her endeavors, to wit, that with her tits and stenography machine and glossy makeup and fine bones she'd one day be discovered by a complainant who would turn out to be a movie producer or publisher of *Ebony* and become some kind of star, then left it at that, went upstairs to my office, and found a slip on my metal desk, like a bit of pink propaganda dropped on the deck of an aircraft carrier, saying "M. Maclarn" called and please call her.

Hey, hi, how's it going. Maisie's throaty voice had—always had had, even when I met her when she was sixteen and even when the words themselves were no more than social boilerplate—an unlikely directness to it. Something about her voice seemed to power her forward, like one of those rocket-propelled personal vehicles the Gyro Gearlooses of the fifties were always inventing. She was going to be in Chinatown and did I want to have lunch. Well really, why wouldn't I, one o'clock, Win Lo.

The crowded downstairs place where I often went, where Joe used to go. Yelling and noodles, din and noodles, as if the noise were so essential a component of the dish that it should take over part of its name. It was a gray day and Maisie had on her long olive coat and coming down the stairs of the tiny shop she looked Irish beyond all reason. Maureen, I called out, and she knew who I meant. Her freckles, her green eyes, her round cheeky face, like a cherub they'd have to keep an eye on. There was barely room on the back of her chair for her coat. I could see it dragging on the tile floor with the used-up napkins and felt oddly sorry for it, for her, as if I could remember a moment in her life when everything was pristine. I offered to put it on one of the hooks, piled up with everybody else's, but she declined, didn't care.

We ordered whatever we ordered and for someone I didn't really know well she looked at me as if I did.

And maybe she was right. We had Sascha's death, after all. I'd been in the car when her sister died in a crash.

"Bobby and I broke up," she said, and when I said nothing because in the group when you didn't know what to say you didn't lean off balance to get words out of your mouth, she said, "He was getting to be too much."

"Oh?"

"He was attacking me."

"Oh no! Poor little defenseless Maisie? Couldn't defend herself?" Amiable and facetious, as though reminding her of the endless course in interpersonal fencing we'd been party to, reminding her as well of the tone of Joe's chiding voice.

"He kept saying he loved me," she said.

I produced a likely-enough grin but what I really felt was badly for Bobby, falling in love with one you weren't supposed to fall for.

Falling in love being to start with our local version of a cardinal sin, most habitual and inevitable and delusional of human behaviors, the mother of all attachments, but being a cardinal sin didn't mean don't do it, but rather if you did it be prepared to observe the consequences.

Sin as descriptive not proscriptive. Sin as warning sign. Sin as something that could waste a lot of your time.

Or, wasting a lot of your time being the very definition of sin in a clocked world, unless of course you learned something from the waste, all rules being made to be broken.

All rules being made to be broken . . . but not all the time . . . Stop. Go back.

"He thinks I'm his mother," Maisie said, and the word "mother" must have hit a flat spot in the restaurant's roar. A guy with an off-duty cop look, mustache and a face like chuck steak, catty-corner from me, looked knowingly my way.

She's an emotional flasher, I thought, Maisie gets off on giving strangers peeks at the fleshy thighs of her secrets.

But I liked that about her, that little sexual *frisson* in her voice as her complaint hurtled past the perimeters of our tipsy little square table into the general communion of elbows and mouths: "I don't like screwing people who think I'm their mother."

"I went out with an Indian girl once," I said, "who insisted that American men only think about their mothers and baseball."

I was trying to be agreeable.

"Exactly! Exactly!" she shouted.

"But I'm surprised about Bobby."

"He's such a baby. I told him to grow up."

"And what did he say?"

"Nothing! *Nothing*! Passive-aggressive. I don't need passive-aggressive in my life right now. Which I also told him."

"Did you tell Joe?"

"Why should I?"

We slurped our noodles awhile, each of us measuring out even breaths because we knew the other one was and sensing sliding noodles down our throats as if we were eating something alive. Once you subtracted to and from, I had only forty-five minutes for lunch, and my glance was already cruising for the guy to get a check when, apropos of what could have been anything at all—we'd been talking about a book about Chinese brush strokes that her own teacher, the painter from New Jersey, was fond of quoting—Maisie asked if I'd ever been in love with her sister.

I sensed my eyes letting in less light, the room getting gray at the edges, as though viewed through an old stereopticon.

"Why do you ask?" I said.

"Don't pull that shit on me. Why do you think I asked? I asked because I want to know."

"Of course," I said, "I had a huge crush on Sascha. I thought you knew that. I thought everybody knew that by now, of the old crowd."

"Everybody loved Sascha," Maisie said, and for a moment her rhetorical wall seemed breached, revealing the rue growing quietly in the garden.

"I guess. Maybe that was so."

As if appealing to it for some unspecified relief, I stole a glance at the greasy Bulova wall clock that overlooked the room like the guardian of its good order.

"Bored? You're bored! I don't believe it!"

"Sorry. Can't piss off the judge. Just a city employee, wage-slave."

We walked through the little park, Chatham Park I think it's called, that separates the courthouse from Chinatown. A Chinese funeral band tramped through in back of us, its tone all the more mournful for its tinniness. Maisie came back to her sister, or rather to the group of us around Sascha, Harry her boyfriend who married her and then she died and then he died in Vietnam, and me and Cord and Teddy Redmond, and what surprised me in Maisie's rendition was that to her we were all the "big kids," Sascha's boyfriend and his roommates from Yale, she didn't distinguish us one from the other. I told her it had never seemed that way to me. Among Harry and Cord and Teddy, who'd known each other since prep school, I'd always felt like the outsider, the "meritocrat" who snuck in, the Jew who'd one day be thrown out. And as if I hadn't deserved to love Sascha, whom a hundred guys had loved, who'd been loved, as they used to say about beautiful girls with dark hair and star-blue eyes who were also rich and smart, "up and down the eastern seaboard"; it was an impertinence, even from afar. Though with Maisie I then corrected myself to add: it had not always felt like an impertinence. At first I loved her sister with the naive optimism of a boy taking on the world, it was only when I got close to her and could compare, the way say an amateur painter might by putting his work next to an old master's, her looks to mine, her style to mine, her family to mine, her charitableness to mine, even probably her mind to mine, that I despaired.

"What do you think about it now?" Maisie's head for a moment facing down.

"It's who I was then."

"When she died . . . it didn't release you?"

"It's all bullshit," I said. "I loved her, but it's all bullshit."

"No it's not," she said.

"That's what I was hoping you would say."

"You're so brainwashed," she said.

"Am I? Or am I just what they say? One person then, one person now, a thousand people in-between . . . I don't know anything."

"You're just chicken to say what you know," she said, and by then we were back on Centre Street.

See you. Thanks for coming. Sorry about you and Bobby.

"You're not sorry."

"I am."

"Thanks for lunch."

"Nada."

"Is the court open to the public? Can I come see you at work?"

"I can't stop you."

"Thanks a lot."

"I wouldn't stop you."

"I don't have anything to do now . . ."

And so it was that Maisie found a seat in the back row of Part AP-5 of Criminal Court in and for the County of New York and watched me do my civil servant wage-slave job for an afternoon.

Although twenty cases were still on the docket and the D.A. had mostly to face the judge, I never quite forgot she was there. If the lawyers approached for a whispered bench conference, I assumed she had to be bored. When I took a plea or made notations on my calendar, I imagined she might note my professionalism. In this odd little world was I not something? A performer on a two-bit stage, anyway, a man without a text.

Go back. Sense. Maisie out there somewhere with little to do of an afternoon, free, of Hodgkin's, of Bobby, one tough cookie Joe would say, who put old slang in everything the same way some men never change from the dress styles of their youth.

And when Diane, on one occasion, shuttled in and out, did she notice? The downtown Helen, cause of strife and shipwreck.

Maisie in this scenario playing Athena.

Go back. Sense. Don't let her steal your attention. Don't let anyone steal your attention. Plea bargain, issue warrants, postpone, argue, bench conference, clear the calendar, pass the time, the end of day.

And when I turned around she wasn't there. I felt a disappointment. A tree that whistles in the forest alone.

Would I always be alone?

Don't get sentimental.

Don't get grand.

Get back.

To where?

Lost.

Sense.

Maisie out in the corridor with the bailed perps and the spit on the floor, having a cigarette, waiting.

"I needed a smoke."

"It was boring."

"It wasn't."

"You weren't bored?"

"That *guy*? That one guy? Who butchered the cow in his apartment?" Her little enthusiasm lighting up the hall.

We walked uptown together. It began to snow, but so lightly it might have been bits of trash swirled by the breeze from the subway. The first bits-of-trash-snow of the season. The darkening crack of Broadway.

She said she loved to walk in the city even though she knew it was a cliché. She who'd grown up on Fifth Avenue, had known the East Side only, then been sent off to school. Summers in Maine, finally Sarah Lawrence, when she'd take the train in and poke around a little, but that was only two years, and now she was learning her native place for the first time.

I can't say that I was attracted to Maisie. Not in the low—or was it comic—way I went for my various Dianes, nor my reverent, impossible love for Maisie's sister. More a comrade than a friend, Maisie made an ineluctable presence. I liked walking with her, talking with her, she'd been away from the city so long it was as though she was from out of town, yet she was one of us without a doubt. One of the Boston cousins, the same language, the same swagger, the same odd tenderness you get from taking on the impossible. Or maybe tenderness isn't the right word, maybe it's more like exposure, like your skin's exposed to something radioactive, something that will burn.

We got up past the loft and kept walking. We were walking just to walk. The temperature was dropping. Maisie's hands in the thin pockets of her coat, her breath blue in the oncoming night, walking slightly faster than I would, setting a pace that had no purpose, businesslike without business, unless the business was to keep the cold at bay, then at Union Square she said, "Fuck it, I'm taking a cab."

"Where to?"

"Home."

"I'll take the train, then."

"You can come with me if you want. You want to come over?"

She was stopped with her hand out into Fourth Avenue, flapping like a frozen piece of fish for a cab.

Going uptown, stuffed in with the foam padding and anti-robbery plex, I had little choice but to look at her a few times anyway. Each time she looked at me back, which was not usual in the group, where theft of attention was always an issue and eyes were often the culprits. Once I thought she was looking at me with pity.

"Just tell me. The black girl who walked in. With the great body? Did you know her? You know which one I mean? She worked there."

"Why do you ask?"

"Would you stop that *shit*, that group-speak *shit*! I want to know if you're fucking her."

"The one in the dress?"

"The one in the dress, yes."

"Not anymore," I said.

"I knew it! I knew it!"

"Bobby told you."

"Told me what? He told me nothing."

"You're just psychic, then."

"I am. I am psychic."

"She was the one the guy beat me up about," I said.

"Well he can eat shit and die," Maisie said.

The Maclarens' duplex was at Fifth and 83rd, across from the museum, Jackie O. country in the argot of the *Post*. They had every sort of art and every sort of rug, yet it was a comfortable place, as though there was so much space they had the luxury of being civilized about it, even casual, anything but grand, no sensors protecting the Seurats and the Monet, no surfeit of maids scuttling around. Views over the dark mounds of the museum, the West Side beyond the trees lighting up its million eyes.

Odd to me then how little impressed I was. In college I'd been in thrall to the rich, the way scholarship boys get. But I was no longer in college and I embraced poverty now, poverty in pursuit of a goal anyway, money being energy for when you needed it and if you were awake you could always get money. Which may not have been true but there were things that I believed. I trailed Maisie from room to room like a slightly bored tourist. But she wasn't showing off, she could have cared less about any of it, it was a place to stay and she was a natural monk. Her parents were on one of those rich people tours of Antarctica, one tablespoon luxury one teaspoon adventure, and in the meantime Maisie let the maids go off, why shouldn't they have a vacation too?

A picture of Sascha on a table in a sterling frame, younger than I'd ever known her, in Brearley then, Maisie said. Maisie stopped beside me. Look. Sense. Sweet saliva on my tongue. A girl I'd never known, dark eyes, intense stare, eyebrows a little thick as if no thought had yet been given to plucking them, the beginnings of a smile. Sascha had never smiled much but she liked to be made to laugh. The girl in the picture with more hope than the one I knew. A virgin? Maybe, probably. Maisie would have been a little girl then.

We said nothing.

The two sisters are little alike, I thought.

The two sisters are much alike, I thought. Their mouths, maybe. Something defiant.

The corners of their mouths a little downturned, Jeanne Moreau-style.

We continued to say nothing until I said, "Tell me about Bobby."

"No I won't," she said. "You only want me to so you won't feel guilty. Because you know what's going to happen now."

"Do I?"

"Don't you?"

"Anyway I won't feel guilty. No matter what, I won't."

By which I meant I'd feel what I already felt, which Maisie understood, broken down into its constituent parts, the queasy stomach, the tight shoulders, the parched mouth, the hot forehead, and words in my head repeating everything I was not and did not believe and did not truly think, for instance that I was a free man and a strong man and strength and freedom were virtue and virtue is truth and my cock is hard and will not only not be but mustn't be denied, the best of all possible worlds and anyway the way things were.

This we might call guilt. These we might classify, anyway, as manifestations of the emotion. But because we don't attach to it, because we let all of it go and see where it goes and don't care and there's still this other "I" somewhere watching it, "I" the observer, "I" the sensing looking and listening guy, "I" do not feel guilt at all.

Ipso facto proved, and you ought to know it, bitch. Do you want to get fucked by a machine? Only the machine feels guilt, it's a product, a result, a mechanism. "I" am free, Maisie. "I" am free. Or anyway "I" am inchoate and a chance and chances have no feelings.

"But what *about* Bobby, then?"

"Tell me," I said.

"Why should I?"

"You yourself just said."

"What did I say? What *did* I say?"

"You are crazy."

"Of course I'm crazy. I was in McLean's."

When I kissed her, I wasn't kissing her sister. I swore I wasn't and it didn't seem like it. Her green eyes, for one thing. And the voice, and her upper arms firm and a little muscular, her skin so white, and the way she knew so much more than I did but different things from Sascha. Sascha never had reason to know much about me, I was a minor island off the coast of her life. Maisie had already shared my mind, along with thirty other birds.

We kissed a couple times more, her lips a little chapped, our saliva on them like a milky balm.

"We could do this or we could not," she said.

"I know."

We let go of each other's fingertips.

Her face grew foreign to me, exuded unfamiliar detail, a jaw, a downy lip, as if she really were some Irish girl I'd just picked up and I had a sudden urge to go home and hide. Maureen? Is your name Maureen?

My name is Maisie Maclaren and I see right through your shit.

Go back. Sense. Her eyes reflecting mine and mine reflecting hers, aqueous, unstable, for a moment almost clear. Love is an action.

Love is kindness, attention, respect.

Love is nothing more.

Now somehow we were in the kitchen and I'd made her an omelet the way Bobby showed me how to make one and she'd poured me more wine from a very good bottle and I asked her about her chemo and her hair, how long it had taken to grow which I thought was a true question but she smacked me in the face.

Pity the poor fella who falls for the wrong sort of girl.

And I wasn't really falling. Not yet, anyway, not now.

"My chemo's none of your fucking asshole business," she screamed at me, as tears streamed down her face. "All right? Okay? A half an inch a month, okay? Okay? My hair."

She was pulling at her hair.

"That's how fast it grows," she screamed, "so do your arithmetic, asshole!"

When she was done screaming, she was kissing me, our cheeks and lips brined with her tears. Sex with Maisie was easy and comprehensive, it lasted as long as we wished and we came or not as we wished and we tore at each other and cried and retreated as we wished and the only fissures in "we" were the ones, for kicks, we allowed: love is an action, love is kindness attention and respect.

Yes? No?

Is "comprehensive" too cold a word for sex?

But it wasn't then.

Yes. Yes. Maisie. Sweet crazy Maisie, whose sister I'd known and loved like a troubadour's apprentice and now I was with Maisie.

Rich girl poor little et cetera with Hodgkin's and short hair and chemo, all better now Maisie.

No liberation in our bodies, but rather the truth that our bodies are with us. We lay where we fell, on a rug somewhere in one of the rooms of which there were too many and I remember on the ceiling there was a little crack like in the *Madeline* book, Maisie pointed it out to me, raised her hand towards it, as if pointing up to God, and I knew what she was talking about.

She loved that crack in the ceiling, she said, it was the only thing wrong in the whole apartment.

It was like a holy idiot, I thought without words, and I told her I thought that without words and she said she was going to tell me about Bobby because she could see I was his friend and she could see I wasn't guilty.

I who, when it was Maisie's sister I'd loved, had never kissed her once nor even tried.

But after Sascha was dead, her husband my friend who knew I had the crush said next time I mustn't roll over, next time I should fight for love.

And ever since I'd been screwing whoever but hadn't been in love and gave up being in love but also gave up certain qualms, in keeping with the common superstition that people grow up or anyway get older.

You must be capable of taking everything. You must prove to yourself you can take everything. For if you're not capable of taking it, how can you truly give anything away?

I said to Maisie, in words more or less, yes, tell me this tale of Bobby my friend that I might hold him close to my heart, in generosity and trust.

But she must have changed her mind again because all she could tell me was that Bobby only liked to fuck her in the ass and she didn't like being fucked in the ass. "He likes fucking his mother in the ass," she said. "Can you believe that? Is that sick or what?"

"But you're not his mother," I said. "Not really."

"You're *so* literal."

"That's not all there is to it," I said.

But she turned away from me. "It's all I know."

"Why did you tell me such an ugly little thing?" I said, "I wished you'd left it at 'He keeps telling me he loves me.'" When I said it I was thinking she was going to bite my dick off but actually she cried.

"Hold me," she said, "just hold me you jerk," and I did.

CHAPTER 9

BOBBY AND I, HISTORY and background.

There was no real rivalry between us. How could there be? In each area where our lives appeared to carry on in parallel, so that comparisons might be made, Bobby was way down the track, so far ahead that we might have been like two of Gurdjieff's worlds, one composed of matter so much finer than the other that the only way the one might appear in the other's perceptual universe was as a sort of shadow, a faint suggestion of its genuine self.

But for a long time I didn't see it that way. Like a nation of modest resources trying to avoid confrontation through diplomatic means, I suppressed my instincts for rivalry by developing the notion that we were complementary figures, the way they sometimes say of partners that it takes both of them to make one good man. I aspired to what I settled on as Bobby's lopsidedness, his loopy brilliance which captured the attention of Joe and Philip and the *New Yorker* and every Harvard kid who ever saw his lamppost, and he, in my jujitsu configuration of it, aspired to my normality. Bobby was one who flaked out on appointments, quit jobs, lost whatever money he had, and rubbed the skin off his knuckles as soon as the scabs from the last time he did it began to heal. None of these were considered adaptive traits for the group's spiritual mountain climbing, so Bobby strove to "grow up." Could I who paid my bills on time help Bobby to "grow up"? Could that have been in Joe's mind when he assigned me to be Bobby's assistant in the kitchen? It dawned on me only in the course of the group's slow expansion, as Joe with his ad in the *Voice* stocked us with all sorts of normal types—he interviewed every applicant and more than once mentioned how he tossed out the "crazies"—that "normality," in terms relative to Bobby or even to me, was not so hard to come by. It represented the norm, after all. Bobby was soon making friends with Big Ronald the commodities trader and Julie the receptionist at Cahill, Gordon and Greg the appliance salesman downtown whom Joe met while buying a new TV. In comparison, I with my Yale apparatus and complicated writing fantasies, the days and years spent in my room feeling superior to most of humankind, hardly qualified as a paragon of "normal." Bobby didn't need my help to grow up. At the same time, he was obviously Joe's pet project. Philip was Joe's ally and confidante, but Joe doted on Bobby.

*

Then what did Bobby need me for at all? He didn't "need" me, but I think he liked me. And it may have been that he had a need for people to like. I was like a throwback to his past, a link to more indolent days. We shared a commitment to one of Joe's principles that others more honored in the breach, namely that one must accept nothing on faith, but only what has been proved beyond doubt to one's own satisfaction. Who was it, which Protestant theologian, said the essence of faith is doubt? Tillich? Niebuhr? Some saint of the twentieth century, some gray name from college, his modernity etched in the makeshift eternity of the trade paperback. I've forgotten so much, I forget nearly everything, the ends of movies, the middle of books, lines of poetry which I claim to love, and the names of the people I met at dinner last week. But somehow not that phrase. Bobby reminded me of it on one of the first walks we took together. We walked, we were *flaneurs* of the spirit, aristocrats of the streets. We still talked about Kierkegaard, for God's sake. Had Joe ever heard of Kierkegaard? Those lines of Baudelaire Bobby quoted to him. Joe was not a learned man. There were moments when I felt with Bobby that we were like medieval monks, storing the learning of the ages for future generations. We were subversives in a way. Joe's theory was that too much interference of the intellect spoiled the chances of the whole Self. And moreover that the chief flaw of our age and place was the over-domination of the intellectual factor. People were thinking themselves to death. No wonder intellectuals were so unhappy. Theorizing and intellectualizing and idle talk untethered to a practice, a tradition, a group, an inner search, a body evolving self-consciousness, were useless. Yet Bobby and I kept talking, about whoever and whatever, again like medieval monks who dedicated their lives to reconciling the Church with Aristotle, trying to find points of contiguity between the group and the world, reassurances, proof.

Of course from another perspective it was Joe who was the true subversive, understanding the whole world differently from most, and Bobby and I were merely trimmers, a reactionary faction, unwilling to commit to what our eyes and ears and hearts told us was so, but which our brains, like the last of the bourgeoisie, resolutely feared.

The Chinese curse, to live in interesting times.

We stayed, week to week and year to year, because of one thing we were certain: otherwise we were doomed.

We had not come to Joe, either of us, until we were disappointed by life.

We continued placing our two dollar bets on the world, playing for the glittering prizes.

But we were seekers after all.

*

He was the one, at the outset, who held his hand out to me. "Why don't you come over to Joe's on Saturday? You might find it interesting."

"Why? What's going on?"

"It might explain a few things."

This at a time when the Thursday evening readings at Philip's were spinning my mind like a top. They had become the highlight of my week, a point of new departure.

Bobby was pimping for Joe, I suppose you could say. But I never saw it that way. Rather, I saw Bobby as my backer, the one who must first have seen my possibilities, who tossed my hat in the ring. Not everyone from the Thursday night readings was asked to come on Saturdays. On account of Bobby I became once again a part of a privileged sector.

*

If there was no true rivalry between Bobby and me, then there was none for the affection of Philip. A syllogism of the distracted. Philip had gotten Bobby his gigs at the *New Yorker*, the cartoons, a couple of Talk pieces, a casual in which Philip wrote the text and Bobby did the drawings. With the *Bird Guide* it was the same. It was as if Philip was grooming him in the literary world just as Joe was grooming him in the spiritual one. As above, so below. Thus my sense of contained miracle the night Philip asked me to write a Talk story with him. It was as if I'd sat in the back of the class waiting to be recognized, or on the bench, a third-string quarterback getting old—but abruptly and with scarcely an explanation in the last quarter of the Superbowl, introducing number thirty-three . . . the PA like a sonic boom, the slutty cheerleaders in a pat routine of legs and flounces.

*

"Maisie and I got together," I said to him the next afternoon at the Sloan's on Eighth Street.

"Go for it," Bobby said. Cheerful and supportive, as if he expected anywhere he went that I would follow, even that it was part of a plan. In accord with the old dictum: you can't advance without placing someone on the step you now occupy. "Has she acted crazy yet?"

I shrugged because I didn't want to say.

"Of course, she's crazy."

"We're all crazy," I replied, feeling uncomfortably manly and full of shit, not believing any longer than it took me to hear my words, their false declarativeness, their reach for the aphoristic, that eliding Bobby's world into mine would somehow patch things up.

"Some more crazy than others. Well, bonk her for me."

Bobby was buying Häagen-Dazs for Joe. He paid with Joe's money, like a child sent to the store. I looked at him as he waited for change. No hint of anything but a resolute goodwill. No negative emotions from this boy. The beginnings of a smile, white teeth.

We came back to the loft and chopped vegetables for most of an hour. Our blades were very sharp that day.

"Don't be embarrassed," Bobby said finally.

"About what?"

"What you were just thinking," he said, but I couldn't think what that was.

*

The provenance of the group.

The Old Painter: studied with Gurdjieff people somewhere in rural Pennsylvania, but also his mother was a Freudian shrink.

Joe: studied with the Old Painter, but also at an ashram in India, which later he called a waste of time. Both grandfathers, rabbis.

Philip: before Joe arrived at his apartment, had been involved with Sufi study groups led by a psychologist at UC Davis who was among the pioneers of "left brain/right brain" thinking, which itself, in certain circles, was held to be a Sufi idea. The psychologist himself was said to have contacts with, or have been acting at the behest or instruction of, a nine hundred-year-old dervish school in Marrakesh that had also opened a "branch" in England. Philip began the story readings in his apartment, as well as the *Bird Guide*, in furtherance of his involvement with the left brain/right brain psychologist, whom he also promoted in various articles, in the *Times* and elsewhere, into something of a national figure.

But once Joe arrived at Philip's, he took over. Sufi stories continued to be read, but with less piety and mysterious conviction, and perhaps with less poetry as well. A strain entered, but never a total break, in the relationship between Philip and the left brain/right brain psychologist.

Thus, many streams made the Ganges.

It is said the teacher finds you and not the other way around.

Sometimes I tried, with arrows, to draw this provenance in my head, searching for reassurance, reliability, the chances of truth. I may as well have been playing tic-tac-toe.

*

Joe on self-understanding:

"Why bother?

"Really, it's worthless.

"It's the most worthless thing in the world. What can you do with it?

"That's one way of looking at it, anyway.

"You have to decide for yourself. One way or another, you have to pay for it. It doesn't come cheap. What are you willing to pay for something so worthless?

"The pearl of great price."

CHAPTER 10

JOE LOVED HIS CHRISTMAS tree as only a kike from Brooklyn could. He shaped it with his Swiss pruners like a patient haircutter confronting an unusually shaped head, clipping tufts and outcroppings, patting and circling and standing slightly back. He fed it daily rations of soluble plant food, little sachets of pink crystals. He doted on its decoration, pulling his Eames chair up and playing Bing Crosby as he sat before it with the blank, well-fed gaze of satisfaction that men in corduroy pants more typically reserve for a crackling fire, as though Joe understood the tree lights to be nothing other than a visual avatar of fire's warmth. Joe whose take on Jesus included prominently the fact that he was a kike like himself, who moreover like himself would not have denied his kikedom even while proclaiming understandings that drove the priests and rabbis nuts. "Only a kike from Nazareth," one in a line of great saints that have appeared here and there throughout the length of human history, but more often than not below history's granite gaze, the difference with Jesus being that he was discovered or remembered, great p.r., whatever. An incarnation, as we all might be if we but knew it, if we could only discover our true selves we would be as little selfish as he, because our self would be other than the false self for which we'd been selfish. Jesus in the abstract, untethered to church, available to all, merciful and not jealous, in some singsong echo of a speech writer's dream asking not for your belief but your understanding. Jesus on the cross?

Okay for those long skinny types but Joe himself would have been too heavy for a cross. It would have taken quite a skilled carpenter of crucifixes, or quite a lot of extra nails, to hold him up there. Or in all events he would not have looked good crucified, his agony would not have got its due, his belly and arms sagging, his face disappearing in his neck, his rotundity zeroing out the cross's stern lankness. No, better if you were Joe to sit cross-legged under a bodhi tree. But it was his Christmas tree that he loved, pagan symbol, clad in the forest's moist and furry mystery, redolent of rebirth, the thing he didn't have as a kid.

Liddie and Big Ronald had gone shopping for it and come back with one ten feet tall. Joe wanted it near the TV, perhaps so that he could always have it in his sight. It was gaudy as hell by the time we were finished with it: good taste and moderation were for us like lapsed aims from another, failed universe, Joe kept exclaiming it didn't look Italian enough, or *now* it looked Italian, kept asking Liddie if it yet looked like a tree out of her Queens childhood, Liddie would nod yes or no, and the tinseling and popcorning and stringing of feathery golden boas, as if it were Mae West we were dressing, would continue. In the group, everything was a lesson, that might return us at any instant to the question of consciousness, and the tree was no exception. Joe insisted that we apply tinsel to it one strand at a time. No draping of handfuls over branches as if in the lazy arrogance of our human power we could bring silver waterfalls instantly into being, no industrialized, sleep-made Christmas tree for us. No, our tinsel would be applied with a Pre-Raphaelite, or Japanese, care, as though we were tending to a forest of bamboo, making sure it was thinned so every tree could be seen. Each strand of tinsel must have its own being. None can lie on top of any other.

This was an experiment for life, after all. This was a training to see, to be. All existence a slender reed, a tinsel strand, a chance, or nothing at all.

Saturday morning, twelve of us over at the loft, myself and Philip and Cal and Bobby and Valerie and Julie and Ty Duncan, Big Ronald, Colin Folger the saxophonist, Laura the barkeep at the topless bar on 33rd Street, and Joe. And Maisie. Somebody had brought doughnuts. Maurice Chevalier on the tape deck now, wry, slightly ridiculous and rouged, like a beautiful pedophile found out, and after Mo a Donkey Serenade and band of faux mariachis. There wasn't room around even so large a tree for all of us to crowd at once, so three or four at any one moment would approach, emissaries in motley hues, reluctant Magi, to lay on our gifts, our sacrificial offerings. All the rest of us using our eyes looking for spots that might love a strand, lifting the tinsel off its cardboard racks as patiently as monks raising a sand mandala, so that not a single strand would be lost.

Essential also to our dance that we used the same boxes of tinsel, the same cardboard racks, that we'd used the year before, and after New Year's we would again remove the tinsel from the tree strand by strand, drape each filament back on the scarecrow cardboard racks, like pants that had been pressed, and place the racks in their flimsy cardboard boxes for next year.

A strand of tinsel adheres to my pathetically pink finger. I sense its feathery embrace, sense the moisture of my finger offering it a tentative adhesion. When I move my hand, the tinsel resists, glinting slivers of wings, blown in the turbulence created by my movement. As if offering the reassurance of accompaniment, I cup my other hand beneath it, I sense the tinsel tickling my palm. I begin to hate Joe for this torture, this absurdity. Why bother with any of it where was it getting me nowhere while the world rushed by people getting ahead it's Saturday for chrissake I could be out shopping. If only I had a little money, which is Joe's fault too though I don't remember exactly how. Stop. Go back. Sense the tree the greeny whispered scent the tinsel borne aloft no fuck you pardon me excuse me but fuck you fuck the tinsel April is hardly the cruelest month the month that is the cruelest month is the month between Thanksgiving and New Year's joy drawn too tight for comfort turkeys tossed across the table domestic beefs murders and cheap toys break. The warm part of Joe, the *heimische* mothering psychologizing part, embraced the worst shit theory of the holidays, to wit that's when the worst shit comes up because that's where it lies. Suffer, you bastards, seek repentance and forgiveness because you can't help but seek them, but follow whatever comes up. Well, I am sick of it now, I am sick of all of it, I will not sense and yet I do, the more easily the more I urge myself not to. I place my tinsel on a lower branch. I sense the bending of my knees, the leaning of my torso. I extend my finger like a docking station to the branch and drop away, leaving the tinsel hung like a silent film comic on a flagpole.

I do my job! So don't ask me *how* I do it! And yet . . . And yet . . . I sense all this. I think I let it go. My rage, that is, if that's what it is, my fight, my defiance, my sadness. It floats off like the tinsel from my finger. It is lighter than air after all. My sense that Joe, too much like my secret self, is embarrassing.

Joe rails about us not having enough tinsel. If we hadn't wasted it and broken it last year, we'd have enough now. If we were conscious, if we sensed ourselves, we wouldn't break it. Now we have to go buy more tinsel and next year we'll have to buy still more, and it could go on and on, forever. Did we expect the group to go on forever? It would not go on forever, he guaranteed us that. It would go on only so long as it was useful, for the time and the place, and then it would be gone. How did we feel about that? What did we sense? Missing mom?

"Work, you bastards. Get this tree fucking decorated!" Joe's meat grinder laugh seeping more subtly into his railing, until, achieving a critical mass of infiltration, it overwhelms it and takes it prisoner.

Were we fools to take him seriously?

He meant no harm.

Zen master's stick.

Joe asked who wanted to go to the dime store for more tinsel and because I was dying to get out I said me.

He retrieved from his pocket a ten dollar bill which he managed to finger so that it folded down lengthwise like an inverted "v." I took it thinking how old-fashioned Joe was, that the provision of cash still inspired flourishes in him. Cash was king when he grew up, when his father had the dry cleaners. Or was the flourish an act too?

"So. Now we know who wants to get out of here."

I sensed myself grinning like a wooden doll, primitive, untutored, with my mouth painted red.

Up until then I'd scarcely paid attention to Maisie, Comrade Maisie my new squeeze, in the room but not of it, tinseling the tree like all the rest of us. Nor had I noticed if Bobby stole glances her way, or if like moons of attraction they came close. I knew she hadn't come close to me, not so that I sensed the heat of her or the sweet brush of her hair. That is, until I was at the elevator my toes pushing into my loafers, and I caught a sidelong glance of her olive coat, flashing and stretching out, like a forest animal waking up. "Gotta go," she said to Joe. "Gotta go uptown." We left in the elevator and I kissed her.

Her saliva as though we'd just met, foreign with coffee and cigarettes and a burnt unfamiliar taste of cinnamon, street girl in the elevator, eyes open and fluorescent-lit, her lips chapped and cool.

As though to beg the question why kiss at all, but in the street she took my hand.

O Maisie what shall we do today, shall we to Banbery Faire, or to Lamston's and buy tinsel?

A break in the weather, in the forties. Jackets loose, people in the shops, bags, bustle, Salvation Army guys, more than enough terror of the situation to go around, dear Maisie, but let us pay it no mind, shall we?

"That's *plenty* of tinsel."

"*This?*"

"Four boxes? Come on. How much are they?"

"Dollar nineteen."

"Plenty."

"Okay."

"Fuck it."

"*What?*"

"I don't want to go back there."

"You don't have to."

"Come with me."

"What about the tinsel?"

"Fuck the tinsel. Really. Let's go home. It's so nice out. You want to walk? We'll walk fast."

One reason not to go back being to test the torque of my resistance, to see how guilty I'll feel.

But why should I feel guilty at all?

"Why should you?" she said.

"I've gone through this before with you," I said.

For profaning my deepest wishes, slighting my seriousness, muddying my purpose, sullying the finery of the ragged cloak that I bring to my would-be self?

"They don't need the tinsel. He's got like what, eight boxes? The thing looks like a lamé dress. Trust me, he will *not* care."

"The devil with red hair made me do it."

The plastic air of Lamston's, as if every product on its shelves were emitting a gaseous residue of itself. Pay for tinsel with crisp ten-spot, get ass pinched by Maisie and I don't know why or if anybody saw.

Walking uptown fast, film of the city speeded up. Like two escaped convicts now, the biggest thing they hold in common their shared escape. Back to Maisie's parents' place where we can fuck on any rug. "You like to defile," I say.

"I think I do."

Reason to fuck her again.

Green eyes and freckles, green eggs and ham. "You're not my type," I say, and she says the same back to me.

"Jewish boys. I don't know."

"Fuck yourself then."

"Go take your tinsel, go, go, they're waiting."

"You said they wouldn't be."

"I lied."

Instead the phone rings and it's Bobby, who knew, he says, we'd be here.

Lying on Maisie's breastbone between her puppy ear breasts, I can hear the cadences of his words like distant calls, of departing trains or planes. Maisie chirpy and easy with him, her husky voice a slather of possibilities. Did he want to come up? What was he doing? What were *we* doing? Just goofing around. It's such a nice day. The tinsel's on hold. She's a bad influence, she's teaching me how to be bad. Sure. Okay. Why don't we just blow this popsicle stand?

Which in the end is what we did. We met him on the steps of the museum. He had on the ratty camel coat, so oversized it made him look like a waif, that he'd bought off a *kif* merchant in Cairo in the vague understanding that a British diplomat from an unspecified era had left it behind. There was no tension to the three of us together. If anything we were closer than we'd been, as if a clingy fatalism, a web spun of erotic vectors, bound us now. Three little lambs who showed no negative emotion, who let everything go. The world is our oyster, we shall not want. Bobby slipping in between us like a brother or a son. Bobby, as well, who could make us laugh just by being there, his sly smile, mustard smear on his lip, eating a hot dog, in his ratty tent of a coat.

Why had I gotten involved with Maisie at all? He must have cared for her so much more, he would have doted on her. Pity is hatred. Do not. Stop. Go back.

Her choice. Maisie's. I'd had nothing to do with it. Had I? We sat on the cold of the stone steps, runaways who were about to be runaways again, pound puppies, call the dog catcher, has anyone seen his cartoon car?

Situation without words. Pale sun filtered through the bare trees. The rivers of museumgoers, their pant legs, the hems of their coats, their shoes roughed by the winter, trickling to either side of us. As if unwittingly revealing something intimate about themselves, their lives from the knees down, neither sordid nor inspired, the workaday parts. We were laconic by then, a mystery to ourselves. "I've got a car," Maisie said, and it seemed like all that needed to be said.

Why?

Because.

It was as though for a little while we were saying to each other, without words, you matter more to me than this group, this process, this Joe and all of it. You matter to me as people matter to each other.

A rebellion that could spread like wildfire, people remembering that they were alive.

But wasn't that the whole point of the group to begin with?

It all felt like a holiday in an Italian movie where you take your girl on the streetcar to the end of the line.

Driving north on Route 9, 9J or 9 or 9W, we were seldom sure which, the old road through the Hudson River towns, Peekskill and Cornwall and Tivoli, the denuded valley of December.

Maisie's father's BMW with low number plates, a four door scooter in black, Bobby in the back seat with the tinsel that I carried with me like my lunch.

By three o'clock the sun was slanty and low. Maisie liked to drive, both hands on the wheel, as though it was all between herself and the road. She passed a lot of slow vans. I fidgeted the dial and found some mournful country station the others seemed to like. All the while finding that the faster we drove away, the easier it was to sense. As though the hardest thing about sensing looking and listening was trying to do it; if you didn't try, it happened easily enough.

But then why do people pass their lives daydreaming?

I remembered Stuart Little, driving north in his little car, looking for Margalo, the bird who flew away.

Choking on the truest moments of my childhood.

I'd grown up around here, for awhile anyway. Westchester suburbs, closer to the city, but we'd drive up this way to look at the trains along the Hudson route and I'd taken this road, as well, with my mother to her parents' upstate when my father went away. We left everything behind.

Go back. Sense. For several seconds at a time my mind is like an empty mirror. I say this to myself, I become aware, in words, that my mind is blank, I rue the words, I go back. This must be a world record, no don't get grand, call it personal best, my personal best several seconds of clarity no words in my head that I'm aware of. Until once again I say it to myself and go back.

Is this not profound progress?

All you need to do is run away.

Bobby's legs up on the back seat like an odalisque. "Hear the boy talk. Hear the boy talk. Can he talk? He can talk."

"What?"

"If you do something, you think, 'I've done something,' right? Big fat whale big sack of mouth swallowing you up. 'You think you *did* something? Yeah. Sure.' What are we doing here?"

"I'm driving. You're sounding like a stoned monkey."

"My mistress speaks. I'm going to shut up."

Which he did for a little while, but he started again. Talking with his hands, but liltingly so, as if conducting an orchestra of himself, Bobby the back seat conductor. "Will the *New Yorker* buy a cartoon of the void? This is an existential question. If the *New Yorker* won't buy it, does it exist? I was thinking, if I made it really cute. A cute void. Acute void."

Trying too hard to have something to say, I said, "You know those maps from when the world was flat? And the ships fall off if they sail too far, it looks like the ship's going over a waterfall? Like that, maybe?"

But it sounded rehearsed, the air around the words controlled and organized.

Bobby a quiet odalisque.

"Make it like a pussy," Maisie offered. "A., pussy sells, b., what's this void shit if not a pussy? You don't hear women obsessing about voids."

"Was I obsessing, glorious mistress?"

"You were, a little."

"Forget voids. Forget it. Forget voids. What about . . . 'Dr. J. and his Flock, or The Cartoonist Goes Into Therapy?' Tune in next week to see how Dr. J. manages to set up what to the untrained eye appears to be a cute little family circle, eliciting from his desperately injured patients their desperate need for approval from him, which he can then, panel two, turn around, they see their transference, they're *cured!* Wow! And now it's the week after next, panel three, and having been cured, all their fears and their hatred, their insecurity, their abject longing all relegated to the harmless closet of non-attachment, they're ready to take on . . . go out and do battle . . . big action sequence . . . special effects . . . Forbidden Planet . . . panels four, five and six . . . the Void! Returned in a new secret guise. Dr. Void, doing battle with Dr. J.!"

A little north of Albany, on whatever road we were on, we found a motel of cabins with electric heaters. It was already late and there was no TV and we'd been eating in the car. There was only one bed, which we knew going in, but Bobby slept on the far corner of it and Maisie I suppose maybe slept a little closer to me than to him, except when she rolled over. Did their feet touch then?

At one or two Bobby sat up like the guy in his favorite John Held cartoon of Christmas in wherever it was, the asylum, the quarantine, the "pest house," and started talking again, as though he hadn't stopped from the car. "But did you know *this*? . . . Joe's got quite a flat ass. Try drawing it sometime. What fools we be! In the course of my apprenticeship have I not gone to the store 617 times, washed 4,112 dishes, cleaned the toilet bowl eighty-seven times, taken clothes to the Laundromat thirty-one times, how did I know all this, am I a mad autistic genius? No, a simple parlor trick, I keep track of how cheap I am. A fine spiritual exercise, the very doing of it supplies you with the proof of its existence. You know what else I keep track of? How many girlfriends I had before. Three. Not including one whore in Pamplona, Spain while everybody else was running with the bulls. On this basis I could say you were my number one, my love. Oh do not quibble over the meaning of love, my love. Let us not demean ourselves with mere words. I know what I meant to you. I'm under no illusions. But in the morning I want a pancake breakfast."

I thought for a moment Bobby looked my way, plaintive, even contrite.

Maisie slept a little closer to me after that.

Rumpled and breathy, we were up early in the dark and found a diner open for the hunters.

We picked up the Taconic Parkway when we could, smooth over hill and dale, and drove south. Bobby sang a song of his own creation, a plaintive recitative, in which he seemed to be apologizing to Maisie. "Mama threw me from a high high building and I landed on your back. Can I put suntan lotion on your soul?" But she was ignoring him now. Driving, both hands on the wheel. Joe was still in his bathrobe when we arrived. I handed him the tinsel and his change. He said, "Thank you" with that old-fashioned flourish where the "k" becomes the first letter of "you," and in general acted as if we'd been gone twenty minutes. Like one of those moments where a postcard's mailed in 1948 and half a century later the post office finds it in some dubious place hiding in plain sight and delivers it with a one cent stamp.

It was a day of NFL playoffs. Maisie left but Bobby and I stayed, and we added to the overdressed tree, one strand of tinsel at a time. My eye found little places. The overcrowding seemed to dissipate. It seemed a miracle how much room there was in the world. Joe watched the football. Nothing more was said about any of it.

CHAPTER 11

IS THERE SOMETHING ETERNAL to be found in each of us or is there not?

And if there is, what price shall we pay to find it?

What price shall we not pay?

Shall we not bet the farm?

And if we're not sure whether there's something eternal in us or if there's not, what shall we do then?

Shall we shut our eyes and assume the worst?

Shall we claim as beliefs things we don't believe?

How else define what's ignoble in man, except by this pitiful sleep, this endless hypocrisy?

We thirty birds were not believers but on our best days we were not ignoble either. On our best days the thought of transcendence drove us on, causing us to endure humiliation, doubt, embarrassment.

Each of us sensing that we must look like fools.

What was it about Joe that made us sense he was a good bet?

His watery eyes, his baritone voice, the easy assurance of his manner when he came to Philip's? His seeming knowledge of "groups," of Rumi, of Gurdjieff? His lineage through the Old Painter? His talent for guessing people's minds? His ability to take Julie's migraines away when no one or nothing else could, the light touch of his fingers, here, there, who could tell how or why, he did it once in the middle of a meeting, oddly like the guy from Saint Vincent's? His laugh, his imperturbability? The fact that others saw something in him?

Some turn loaves into fishes. Others turn our perceptions of loaves and fishes.

He did not hold any of us prisoner. We might have walked away.

But did any of us have a better bet for saving our skins, or if not our skins our souls, or if not our souls then something unnamable, that was nonetheless in us?

*

That which senses, looks and listens.

That which is everywhere, so that if we sense it deeply enough the barrier of our skin seems to lessen, it's still there but it isn't so fatal, there's more and still more of us, we are everywhere, you could not kill us with a stick.

Though someday the universe may run down. Even the scientists will tell you that.

But if it runs down, will not Brahman breathe again?

In breath, out breath.

What had we to lose, really? A house in the suburbs, cars and money, assumptions, conventions, beliefs, unhappy histories with parents, the sadness of sickness without friends, sexual urges that hardly knew they were alive, that were as atrophied as everything else?

Stop. Please. Listen to me.

We were not crazy.

Quite.

Though "we" may have been the biggest myth of all.

*

Gurdjieff said the ways of escape were four. The way of the monk, which was the way of faith. The way of the yogi, which was the way of mind control. The way of the fakir, which was the way of physical transformation. And the way of the sly man.

*

And whether he was right or not. And who cared whether he was right or not.

But we were in our twenties and God was dead and we were looking to make the best of it.

*

The cult of the individual.

The curse of the individual.

The chance of the individual.

Like mountaineers roped to one another.

*

It is possible to be an atheist. It is possible to believe in the finality of death.

*

It is possible to believe in alchemy. It is possible to believe in any damn thing.

*

But don't go crazy. Go back. Look. Sense.

The world is all around us.

They say the New Age died, but we were never "New Age." Go away with your astrology and veggieism. Go away with your acid. Go away with your droopy hair, hard rock, counter cult, pop cult clichés. Go away with your touchy-feely. Go away with your tendency to blab everything.

A few good men wanted. No bullshit. A few women as well.

*

My favorite quotation of all, the most pertinent, the one to hang on a wall, a ballplayer said it: "It's great to be young and a Giant."

*

When will I write my Talk story with Philip, about the angel of Saint Vincent's?

When will I fuck Maisie again?

When will I be sick with envy over this and that?

When will I ever see Joe as neither good nor bad nor good nor
evil nor yes nor no nor anything but that he is and I am and we are?
Love is what, say again?
Transcendence, bud.
All about transcendence.
You don't want it, don't pay your two dollars.

*

And the millennial edifices, the great religions, the work of the
blood and piety of billions: how dare stand up to those?
We weren't standing up to them. We were sneaking into their
secret heart.

*

Say again, why Joe?
Because he was there.
Because he flattered us, or we imagined that he flattered us, that
we might be there too.
Because we worried that we weren't "there."
Because once you start on something and make friends and your
life gets used to its new assumptions, it's hard to leave. Even the habit
of being unhabitual is hard to give up.
Or because we still believed in Santa Claus?

*

A bird in a cage longs for freedom. It falls down and plays dead.
Its owner opens its cage to remove it and the bird flies off.

Margalo, Stuart Little's love?
Not quite, perhaps, but close enough.

*

O do not say we are alone.

CHAPTER 12

JOE ON PIETY:

"Don't trust the pious ones. They're full of shit. Maybe that works in some places. But not in New York. Here we muck around. Here we go down in the plumbing.

"I look at one of the pious ones, all their talk about 'enlightenment.' What I usually see is anger, hatred, fear. Unacknowledged, of course.

"Give me a good hater. That we can work with.

"And don't talk to me about 'enlightenment.' I hear that word, I want to go take a bath."

CHAPTER 13

IT WAS THE DAY before Christmas, we were in my apartment, behind the robbery gates, on the narrow bed, she was on her side with her head propped on the faded corduroy pillow we'd borrowed from my writing chair, and Maisie said let's masturbate.

Her hand reached between her thighs and rested there, in the folds of the dark fabric of her skirt. "Can you do it without fantasizing?" she said.

"I can't do anything without fantasizing," I said.

"Okay, but mostly not fantasizing."

"I'll try, Maisie. Just for you."

"Really, it's better. You'll see."

"Jesus. Miss Patronizing Bitch."

"I thought you didn't know."

"But I do."

"Then take off your pants," she said, in a way that was sharp like some kitschy prison guard in a porn movie yet sweet and coaxy enough.

I took off my pants and she pulled down hers, we hadn't touched each other once.

"How should we do this?" I said.

"Are you stupid?"

"I mean, should we do it together? Should one of us go first? Should we look at each other? Are we supposed to get excited by each other, or just by the physical sensations?"

"Good questions."

"So high and mighty. So quick to fly off."

"Okay, okay, you made your point."

"I say . . . you go first."

"I say you."

"Why me?"

"Because. Men always come first."

"Is that a joke?"

"You don't have to *come*, you know. You don't have to *get off*. Didn't you ever hear of seminal retention?"

"I like to come."

"Do you use spit?"

I did use spit. But I hadn't always. Spit came with the group. "Try spit," Joe said once, not to me, but I did. And I found that spit had many virtues. It brought you close to your body, you could smell its breathy, mucousy odor on your hand, it was all-natural, it was free, it left no residue, it was slippery wet in a way that even "love oils" were not, and there was plenty of it, the more excited you became about anything, the more of it you produced. Spit in a way being emblematic of what to us masturbation was about: if you want to love others, love yourself first; practice on yourself. And if you want others to love you, don't go to them needy, go to them with a belly well-fed and a spirit bright with satisfaction. People smell neediness and run away. People are too weak to love others' weakness. Masturbation, as well, an opportunity to discover the secret workings of the flesh, the glands, the nervous system. And what else, anything else? Independence, self-reliance? The refutation of old, false shibboleths that were society's propaganda? If you jerked off dry, less tactile pleasure, fewer nerve endings, were available to you, so you were more likely to fantasize, substitute memory and image for sensation, put a veil between yourself and your body.

I told her I used spit. She put her fingers to her tongue and wet them. She was businesslike, she was doing nothing to excite me, she was looking at her hand which glistened pinkly. Her legs lay apart like logs. All of this could have happened in a hospital bed. I couldn't see at first where she placed her fingers. All I could see was the movement of her wrist, flapping motions, rhythmic but not urgent. I began to hear her fingers slosh around then she brought them back to her mouth for more spit. I turned myself around so that I could see between her legs. She raised her knees up. Her labia were dilated and scarlet. She resumed stroking at the knot of their convergence. An easy enough thing to hold my eyes' attention, but could I remember to sense my arms and legs and to listen? Stop. Go back. Gently. Sense. I wasn't sexually aroused.

For a moment I wondered what Maisie must be feeling. Why did I wonder this and what business could it be of mine? I could not know. Maisie less than others. Comrades do not know one another, comrades have too much respect to penetrate the veil or was "comrade" one more excuse for my pitiful isolation?

What? Who says? Whose pitiful isolation? *Our* pitiful isolation. The world's pitiful isolation. Not me, Jack, don't count me in or out.

Her torso slightly arched now, tensed, like a bridge in the wind. Her jaw hard and her lips apart. I could see Maisie's tongue. What phenomena were these that I observed? How piece them together in a narrative of love?

I didn't ask. I declined to ask.

Looking up at her from below, a landscape of hills and dales, nostrils of fire.

Different angles, Maisie, I see you from different angles, Maisie the tigress, Maisie the mountain, Maisie the *kore* lying where she fell, millennia ago, dreaming of her Buddha-boy.

When she made a noise, it was funny, really. The word closest to it being a squeak, Maisie squeaked like something you hear alive in the walls of an apartment, then her fingers went down like miners into their hole and stayed there and when they came out, slow and warm, she was as quiet as a vigil.

Her eyes settled on me without eros or even curiosity, but only as though to say: so what did you see? Her green eyes the eyes of a fish, quiet and ancient.

Are you, did you, I said and hesitated, not being very smart.

For a moment then, and I didn't know why, but my vision expanded until we were both in a picture from Delft or Rotterdam. "The Artist and His Model." "The Studio." "The Quiet Morning." A curl of satisfaction, as if after love, in the girl's smile?

For a moment there was so little to separate us.

And yet still I had no idea about her. All I had was a picture.

Your turn, Maisie said, as if I didn't know.

Portrait of the Artist as a Young Self-Pleasurer, though I was feeling no pleasure then, but rather the anxiety of performance before an audience of one.

Had I not always been a prude? Had I not always feared embarrassment? I remembered these accusations then, though not where they came from. Perhaps they came from nowhere.

Go back. Gently. Sense.

I mustn't let her steal my attention. I mustn't let my hand my eye my dick go to her.

Maisie in repose, her green eyes the eyes of a fish, so what will she see?

I did not want her approval.

Of course I wanted her approval.

But why did I want her approval?

I felt insane, a child's mind in a child's body in a world where people were supposed to have grown.

What happened to me? Why was I left behind?

Maisie help me kiss me adore me. No.

Stop. Go back.

She is here but so are the walls, so is the number five bus outside, its diesel heaves, its downtown passengers going up or maybe its uptown passengers going down, its bus driver with her ham sandwich in the bag behind her back.

Go back. Gently. Sense. Arms. Legs. The world.

Maisie a little light station in its midst but do not be blinded, do not cry, be a man.

Why jerk off?

Why not?

Go back. The wash of guilt. A wave and then it flattens on the beach.

A wave that recapitulates every wave that's gone before.

I put my fingers on both sides of my tongue, as if holding it, as if in command, as though it is more masculine for my fingers to take than my tongue to give, as though this choice of the greater masculine might stand in mitigation of the act. Spit on your fingers is for girls. Spit on your fingers is for sex.

Nevertheless my tongue summons up more of it, sucking on the front of my palate as if in a silent mating call.

My fingers smell of my shame.

Are you crazy? You've deep-ended now.

Go back. Sense.

My hand the center of the picture, pale and wet like Maisie's. Maisie in the room somewhere.

My hand grips my penis which is soft as a boy and cool. At first my hand senses it more than my penis senses my hand, but this changes, and as my penis coalesces in the slippery exchange of rhythms they start to dance with one another, they look equally into each other's eyes.

I bring more saliva to the party.

My penis, like a land creature returning to the sea, swims happily in it and is quiet.

I am beyond guilt's reach now. I've gone offshore, at least for a while. I look at the ceiling, looking for patterns of the ocean in the puddles and lines of the plaster fixes.

I refuse pictures of sexual enticement. Returned to sender, gone. In order to keep them out, my mind's voice counts. I take my breaths as the rhythm of my hand. In out in out up down up down four strokes for every in breath four strokes for every out.

Do not break ranks do not give in to tits and ass.

Tits and ass can watch from the side. Green eyes can watch from the side as we march past, in breath up and down up and down out breath up and down up and down.

How martial. How boring. No, how brave. I have an aim. I will not let sex intrude.

I sense the blood running in my arms and legs. I sense my neck and shoulders tighten. Relax. Go back. Let them go.

Now my blood slows? I think it does. And my nostrils relax and my jaw and my toes, which wriggle as I keep jerking off.

Whoever can jerk off and chew gum at the same time please stand up come forward for your prize.

Here I am. It's me. Remember me?

Little me?

I can jerk off and drop my blood pressure and chew gum and relax my jaw and wriggle my toes even while I move my breath in and out in breath and out breath up and down in and out around and about.

My penis loves me now. My penis wants no other.

You narcissist, you devil.

In out in out in out in out. Breaths as clipped as a soldier's speech.

Maisie in my peripheral vision, a cheerleader, a friend, as neutral as the bed.

I can do this! I can fucking do this!

I sense my spine or try to. Is it there? Do I really have one?

My spine the bearer of my hopes, the old electric eel.

My body prepares. To see what will happen, like the men at Alamogordo in their concrete bunkers with their dark glasses but no, I'll stand up, I'll throw my glasses off I'll be part of the experiment I'll be neither subjective nor objective neither here nor there, in the center of it I sense my forehead.

O do not sense your cock. O do not sense your cock. Sense everything else and your cock will take care of itself I swear I'm not making this up.

Maisie. Quiet. Go back.

I see what help she is now. I remember her and I remember to go back, remember to sense. It's true what they say—the conscious keep each other alive.

Stop. Don't say this. Don't say anything don't think anything. Sense. Arms legs penis spine something in the middle of your head a little towards the front. What's this? What's its name? Don't ask its name. Go back. Sense. No words. Not even the words "no words."

And who shall choose the end of it? Shall my penis or shall "I" and who's "I" anyway?

Yes, "I." Yes, I.

That thing in the middle of my head a little bit towards the front that has so many names but no name at all that thing is it not like the bell at the county fair at the strong man's booth where you get a mallet and pound something on the ground and the something flies up on a pole and if you're really strong the something will fly so high on the pole it will ring the bell whereupon praise will befall you and grace and honor and the love of the carny girls.

The eternal return of the hero give me a break go back sense no words anything but words.

"I" decide I decide enough of this Maisie must be getting bored it's time to get on with the day all experiments must come to an end like good things go to heaven in out up down saliva enough for this slippery world my cock my love go for it faster yes no words.

I am lurking inside my head. "I" am lurking inside my head when the sparkling sweetness comes my way, the restorer of worlds. What has my cock to do with it, or "my" cock, is it not but a switch, a mechanical device? We're talking electricity here, we're talking the spark of life, immeasurable. Sweetness settles over my shoulders over my body like a cloak, power crowns me, or "me," or whoever.

It is all in your head, it is all in your mind. What you sense in your cock is but a pale reflection of what is.

I feel dissolved. "I" feel dissolved.

No words. Fire gone out.

Maisie's over there smiling her fish-eyed smile, *kore* girl carved in stone, waiting for her Buddha-boy.

There's come on my fingers, warm, overpainting such saliva as is left. She hands me my underpants to wipe myself off.

So there's that but it's the day before Christmas so there's also Christmas shopping to do. Back downtown, Canal Street, Mott, the Bowery. Because of the "event" after Christmas, I've taken the whole week off, Chinatown is thronged, with fifty dollars in my pocket I feel rich. Shopping for myself, shopping for ourselves, because this too is part of the work, to bathe ourselves in another kind of love, until the water of the bath is the same as our insides and when we get out we don't know we're gone. Jerk off and buy presents for yourself and defend yourself if attacked. That's the kindergarten course, the one that breaks everything down to its simples. Compassion is so much more advanced, helping others, fucking others. Heal thine selves, would-be physicians of the world. So in Chinatown I buy a cleaver for myself, smooth-grained handle and carbon blade, sufficient to chop the head off a chicken or anything else and I feel I've committed a metaphorical act; added an extension to my hand, a worthy gift, proper to Bobby's assistant in the galley, a workman who does not quarrel with his tools but rather cossets them and oils them, a cleaver such as Joe might have bought, and at seven dollars what a deal. I joke around with Maisie about getting it gift-wrapped. It would slice through the paper, slice through the box, get loose in New York like King Kong. Maisie in her olive coat on a day that looked like rain, seeming happy after our morning together though what the "together" part of it meant I wasn't sure. Lunch in the dim sum joint on Doyers. She's chirpy, we need to buy stuff for the "event," she says, they did five days nonstop in Somerville and everyone brought cushions for their ass and candy to sneak in here and there. You had to prepare for it, it was like a campaign, and what about kneepads for your knees? I said I dreaded the whole thing but she said it wasn't so bad, though seven days would be twice as bad as five. I said to her, not looking her way, that we were like Tristan and Iseult, only in a kind of weird and reversed way, we kept a sword between our emotions while our bodies did what they liked.

A cleaver, Maisie said, is that what you bought the cleaver for, to keep between our emotions?

I said I didn't know.

"It was all just a deception anyway, that Tristan thing?" she asked. "Wasn't it? The sword? Just to fool the king?"

And that's more or less when it started, when I had the inkling that if I looked at her once more, despite all the prohibitions and cleavers galore, I would begin to fall in love with her. I sat slantwise to our little table so that in the frame that my eyes most readily concocted she was little more than a hint out at the eastern border, but hint or no, there she was, her freckled face and know-it-all eyes, her red hair not fully grown, like a fledgling not quite ready to fly. On Bowery at the only store of the time, maybe anywhere in the country, that stocked goods from "Red China," Maisie bought toothpaste and soaps and a comb, and flimsy kneepads for both of us in case we wound up sanding the floor. I tagged along with a curious eagerness, as though watching her shop was like watching something more intimate by far than a couple hours before when her hands had found her vagina. I'd never seen her sister shop. I'd come to think, in an odd way, that rich girls never shopped, not for toothpaste anyway.

Though how long had it been since I even thought of Maisie as rich? Even in her parents' apartment, she seemed like a squatter, a beggar.

But now I did. Maisie bought a lamp for herself, a gaudy tin-seled thing, antidote to everything she'd grown up with, something fabulous, wasn't it fabulous, she kept saying, a lamp, as it were, to go with Joe's Christmas tree, a Chinese outlier of it. We dodged and slipped our way through the last minute crush of humanity up Mott Street, then west on Canal, stopping to look at the fishmongers' wares. This rich girl who gave it up, this rich girl who moved on, to crazy and beyond.

Up Broadway a guy had books on a cart. We were walking by and I felt Maisie beside me, comrade Maisie who could walk fast and in step with me or I in step with her, and I must have glanced because I always glanced at what booksellers had to sell, an unbro-ken habit, a lust for the bargain, transformed, perhaps, into a search for the miraculous at three ninety-eight or less, but in all events there went my eyes, to a facsimile of Blake, the Songs of Innocence and Experience, with Blake's own engravings, printed probably in Hong Kong, black cover with drawing of Tyger Tyger burning bright, wrapped in cellophane as though it were Henry Miller.

How much, I said to the guy and the answer was eight dollars and I would have argued with him but Maisie hadn't seen me yet nor did I want her to she was a couple steps ahead, so I handed him even change and he put the Blake in a brown bag. Blake being some-one from "before," somebody Joe never mentioned and might actu-ally have thought was a crazy old coot, yet despite what I was already imagining as Joe's narrow-mindedness, wasn't Blake apropos? I felt if I gave this to Maisie now I would be giving her a piece of my whole life. I felt also I'd be doing a subversive thing, *ex parte*, private, play-ing a hunch. By then she was up the block, half turned towards me with her hands in her pocket, not really impatient but not patient either, and I thought she looked just fine. As soon as I caught up with her I gave her the bag. "Merry Christmas," I said, as flat as I could. Throwaway Christmas, throwaway gift, downplayed to death, yet there it was. She brought it out.

"What's this?"

"Just, uh, saw it. I don't know."

"Great, it looks great."

"Do you like Blake?"

"Sure. I mean, sure."

"Did I break a rule?"

"Which rule?"

"Buying you a present?"

"No."

She turned the book over. The back of the jacket was a sheet of black. She didn't take the cellophane off, but rather put it back in the bag and put the bag in the bigger bag with her lamp, and we walked along. Her smile went blocks ahead of us, distant and knowing, a smile I hadn't seen quite, but it had mystery and seeming courage.

"What possessed you, young man?"

"Affection."

"Whatever happened to the sword? Excuse me, the cleaver."

"Your esteemed self has caused me momentarily to fuhgeddaboudit."

"Uh-huh."

"Why 'uh-huh'?"

But she didn't say. Though of course I knew what she could have said. A tidy lecture on non-attachment or mom.

"I love Blake," she said instead.

"You're not angry?"

"Surprised."

"No big deal."

"Thanks, though."

"Nada . . . I just thought . . . I mean you were the one said drive to the country. You're the one reminded me of my other life."

"Other lives?"

"Probably . . . I don't know."

"If I say I like you, that's stealing your attention, right?"

"I don't know. Is it?"

"If I say 'I love you' . . . ?"

"Stop. Go back. Sense."

"I am. Maisie . . ."

"Hmm?"

"Forget I said any of it. An experiment."

It was like, I thought, when you try not to sense, there it is. When you try not to fall in love, there it is. Maisie who was all at once on Broadway as it began to rain, the one.

"A gift can be one-sided," I said.

"I have to go to the loft."

I was glad because she sounded rueful.

"What about our secret life?"

"What secret life? Which one?"

At Bleecker in the narrow alcove that smelled of rain and urine, backlit by the white buzzer with Joe's name on it, I kissed her. Her lips parted a little and I touched her hair. She pressed the buzzer.

"You know I don't really want the book," she said.

Still in its bag she removed it from her bigger bag.

"Oh?"

"Sorry?" Her shrug. "Do I have to explain?"

"Of course not. . . . Okay, fuck it, who cares?"

I took it from her and threw it across Broadway, over the hedge of pedestrians narrowly missing a cab landing in the blotchy roadway most of the way across.

"Better?" I asked.

She shrugged again.

Someone was buzzing her up now. Probably Joe, from the length of the buzz.

"See you later," she said.

I nodded.

She went in and I turned my back on her as the elevator doors wiped her away.

Car after car, by now, their windshield wipers going, were running over the book. I could see it out there, as squooshed as any cat, small impediment to the city's flow.

I hated walking in that rain.

Life's an experiment, I said in words to myself, and told myself to shut up.

CHAPTER 14

LOVE AND RELATED ETHICS. Troubadour Sufi Persian Arab Chinese Indian Song of Songs go hither and yon what will you learn about love?

What will words provide?

The Beloved. Neither this nor that nor anything else.

In the grace of the Beloved's gaze.

In the night of the Beloved's absence.

Unsayable ecstasy unsayable sorrow.

The Lover. You. We. I.

What will the Beloved's face look like?

*

Whereas I pitiful I pitiful you pitiful we, the poverty of our little scrawls.

*

Distance.

*

May we glimpse our own pathos, finally?

*

The human face the metaphor of the Beloved's.
Is this deception?
Is this sacrilege?
Or, possibility?

*

Drunkenness.

*

A whiff of perfume.

*

Madness.

*

The scent of roses.

*

The poet under his tree, in repose . . . is he asking or is he telling?

*

Her number at her parents' apartment was a 2-8-8. BUtterfield 8. One of the old-time exchanges. O'Hara's novel. Liz Taylor in the role.

I phoned her. Feeling an unanticipated need to speak with my co-conspirator. I decided that's what I would call her, if I spoke with her, my co-conspirator. But I knew she wouldn't be there. I phoned the BUtterfield 8 number six or seven times, on each occasion feeling more compelled, as if I was beginning to lose my nerve. And what would I have said to my co-conspirator if she was there? Propose, with the stately, measured cadence of a conscious being, an early evening fuck? That would be nice. That sounded sweet. 2-8-8, BUtterfield 8, as if a telephone exchange could be endowed with sensuality. Despite all my best intentions, I was sorry Maisie wasn't there. It was only when I'd finally moved my attention off her, in favor of unwrapping my cleaver, oiling it, feeling its rough-hewn Chinese blade with my fingertip as if preparing for a life's work, that she called me.

"Hi."

"Hey."

"So . . ."

I never got to calling her my co-conspirator. Her voice had that sandpaper taste again.

"Something's wrong."

"What?"

"My glands are swollen."

"Are you sure?"

"Don't patronize me."

"Did you call the doctor?"

"I'm going to talk to Joe"

"But did you call the doctor?"

"Of course I called the doctor. He wasn't there."

"It's Christmas Eve."

"It is."

"Okay then I won't ask you about it."

"What could you ask?"

"Oh come on Maisie—are you okay?"

But her larger point was true enough. What I knew about Hodgkin's disease you could fit into two sentences. Something about stages. Maisie was Stage 2, which wasn't so bad, but the next stage if it came was.

She repeated that her glands were swollen and asked if I knew what that meant and I guessed that I did and said so and asked her which glands.

Her neck, she said, had I noticed her neck?

"I did, actually."

"Today?"

"Uh-huh."

"Because you were looking to see? Because something looked wrong?"

"No."

"You just liked my neck."

"Yes."

"You romantic."

"Maisie—"

"I'm not asking you to think about it, understand? I don't want you to think about it. That's why I never talk about it. I'm not even supposed to. It's bad for me. People like you. Treating me like a freak."

"Okay. Fine."

"Not that you are. I didn't say that you did. You don't."

"Can I come over now?"

"No."

"Are you sure?"

"I'm still at the loft."

"Will I see you later?"

"At Philip's."

"Maybe there's another doctor you can call."

"I don't think so."

"Well—"

"This is my business, okay? I'm sorry I called. Really. It was stupid of me."

And maybe it was, I thought, when she hung up. My co-conspirator.

I went over to the New Yorker bookstore then. Thank God for Jews and secularists, open on Christmas Eve. I wanted a book on Hodgkin's disease. I would read up and make myself useful to her or anyway know better who, or what, I was confronting. But I didn't think her glands were swollen. They hadn't looked swollen to me. I thought she was simply afraid.

CHAPTER 15

PHILIP'S PARTY ON CHRISTMAS Eve was from midnight to
dawn. It was hardly billed as a party. More like a refuge for orphans,
strays and insomniacs. People sat on the floor and played board
games or read the Sufi books or quietly talked. Almost nobody stood
around. Nobody milled. The single room of Philip's apartment held
us in a kind of suspended elegance, as if it were a hatbox. It was a
room seeded with his childhood—models of locomotives, train
timetables, books on baseball, stamp albums and a Scott's catalog—
but at the same time, with its frayed leather armchair and faded wall
paint of indeterminate color, grayed further by the mysterious ema-
nations of a negative ionizer, it breathed the composed disarray of a
college room, say an American dream of Oxbridge. The archaeol-
ogy, the layered cities, of a boy. As well, for me, it was the room
where I'd first come to meet these people. It held the feeling, as much
as anyplace, of home for me, despite we, the group, having come in
and built Philip bunk beds and a redwood deck, spiffing the place

up beyond the previously supposed boundaries of Philip's taste, even giving him an ostentatiously lordly perch over the backyards of 12th and 13th Streets. Two short birch logs burned innocuously, with steady indifference, in the fireplace. Philip greeted each guest with a glass of hundred-proof bourbon, which they didn't have to drink, nobody was making Russian toasts with it, but it was there anyway, part of a stash he'd acquired doing a Talk story on a New Yorker who'd become a master distiller in Louisville, offered now both as sacrament and sacrilege: all hurt feelings welcome here.

I sat down to play cards with Big Ronald, Matthew Fellner, Laura and Julie. Poker for pennies, the kind of game where the girls had a cheatsheet which they passed back and forth showing what beat what, which still didn't keep Julie from asking every ten minutes or less what a straight was or the difference between a straight and a flush. I liked Julie, in the old college phrase she was tough, lanky with a turned-up nose and nasally Five Towns accent. She and Matthew had been together for years, he was a rich kid from Great Neck, one step up the nouveau ladder from her, they drove a Suburban now but before the group they'd lived "alternatively" in Crested Butte, from which she'd brought back, like the proverbial pearl of great price, an amazing chocolate cake, succor for the long stoned Colorado winters, composed of every impure ingredient to be found in the local co-op, cake mix and instant chocolate pudding and Crisco and bags of chocolate chips and whatever else, an example of which she'd provided this night, to go with the card games and the bourbon. We all believed in sweets, as metaphor and remembrance. People who didn't believe in chocolate were afraid of being sweetened themselves. But what was I doing with Julie and Matthew? Were it not for the group, they'd never have been my friends. They were bland, their jobs were boring, they could do me little good, although Julie's tits were nice. The old analysis, the pre-group analysis, of the "power-mad rat" that had been me and was still me most of the time. The same with Big Ronald, the commodities trader from Okieland. Ronald was a rascal, he'd blown up bridges in the Peace Corps in the High Atlas, he cared about money, he actually had kids, a couple of them from a down-home marriage. I had no idea, really, what had brought Big Ronald to the group, but there must have been something in him, something unsatisfied, breathing through a straw, buried under the burlap twang and toothy smile. Or, he'd been going out with Laura. Maybe Laura had brought him. It was often that way. You came here on account of a squeeze and then you didn't want to leave. Laura'd been an office manager, until the job at Cowgirls East came up. Putting on his avuncular career counseling hat, Joe had said try it maybe you'll like it, and she had, and she did, the girl camaraderie, the guys with their hard-ons. She broke up with Big Ronald, who then screwed Liddie for awhile and after Liddie he said he was tying a rubber band around it. Were these my people? They were now. I was finding it easy to sense this night. Being with others who were sensing, doing nothing much. The room seemed to glow, as if we were in a set designer's gaslight. I was losing, as usual, at cards. No real fighting spirit, nor skill. Julie wanted to win and cheatsheet or no she was doing it, yelping less ironically than we cosmopolitans might have hoped for each time she hauled in a pot. Sense. Look. Listen. But as we played, the words in my head grew denser and more consistent, until eventually I could recognize in them a theme of surprised self-satisfaction. I was not unhappy to have Big Ronald, Matthew, Julie and Laura as my friends, I was not unhappy to be wasting my time playing cards with them. Wasting time, consciously wasting time, an unexpected badge of pride; worthless friends, consciously worthless, a badge of superiority. And what was this "worthless" shit? Worthless word, worthless words. Worthless workers of the world unite, save me from a world of ambition and snobbery. Escape from my falsest self. Here, family. Here, friends. Here, the vain world is seen for what it is and we laugh. Even I laugh, who hadn't laughed enough. Sitting now in the card-playing embrace of the solid, the openhanded, the less deceived, the sort who might dedicate their lives to something and stick with it to the bitter end. For a few moments I saw Big Ronald and even Laura as I imagined Joe must see them. Good seed, good soil. Until with a kind of garish, urgent rush I recognized the pride I felt at being with them as no better than the pride that might have led me to ignore them, it was all pride, all the same, all of it keeping me from what is. Words. Hallucination. Go back. Gently. Sense.

All my bullshit schema. All my theories. All my self-criticism. What did they get me?

Confusion.

Go back.

I drained the bottom of my cup of bourbon. Its warmth, the room's warmth, my friends' warmth.

All is forgiven.

How could it not be forgiven?

Forgiveness as organic, as what is.

Go back.

The sweetness of the bourbon. The sweetness of Philip, of his boyhood.

Laura's tits, Julie's tits. The sweetness of these too.

Where's Maisie? Where's Bobby?

But Maisie was supposed to be here.

Moments later I wasn't sure if I'd begun to think this last thought of Maisie before the doorbell rang or after.

Could my unconscious not hear the ring before my conscious mind?

Wasn't that how precognition worked?

It wasn't Maisie at the door, nor Bobby. I cranked my neck to see whoever Philip was greeting, a bundled shape smaller than himself. "You made it. Come in. Look who's here." Philip waving at me like a bandmaster, as the guy from Saint Vincent's took a couple steps across Philip's threshold, a little bit tentative, a little bit shivery, as if he was happy to be out of the cold but not sure if he'd really come to the right place. It was a quarter after one and for a second I took him for Santa Claus, the Santa of the old black-and-white movies anyway, the one that came in unusual guises.

Some patchy back-and-forth with Philip about his name, which was Joao, which Philip already had to know, since he'd called him to invite him. Philip offering him bourbon, offering him chocolate cake, taking his coat and still flagging me over, never chirpier than when he was gracious, like the kindest chipmunk on earth. When Philip threw a party he had a tendency to invite anyone he ran into for weeks in advance, but there were none outside the group who could be counted on to show up after one or two in the morning. What had Joao been doing? What did he imagine? It was a long ways from Sao Paulo. He had on a thin acrylic black sweater, he'd oiled his hair, and he held in his hand a small square box wrapped with a single dark-colored ribbon which he'd retrieved from his coat pocket before Philip whisked the coat away. Forthrightly, as though embarrassment wasn't part of his nature, Joao handed the box over and Philip fussed about it, opened it with quiet ceremony to find inside a key chain with a picture of Pelé set against the flapping green of the Brazilian flag. Philip poured Joao his ration of bourbon. Joao recognized me as soon as I got up. "Okay with girl now?" "No more

girl. No more girl. Different girl." The pleasures of pidgin, allow-
ing each side to think it's doing its best.

Philip asked Joao if he felt like talking about Saint Vincent's,
because wasn't now as good a time as any, and Joao, who knew
phrases, said why not. Why not, why not—why not me do the interviewing, Philip said, Louie could do the interviewing, if Joao
didn't mind. Why not?

There was something about Joao that put him not out of place
with us. Even I had discovered that in a room full of people trying
to stay in the present the one who wasn't, who was clueless and flying all over, would stand out, as if he was fighting the room or oblivi-
ous to it. But Joao didn't stand out. Who knew, was it his
faith-healing or his simple modesty or was he a secret Sufi saint? In
a corner of the room, out of the way, I interviewed Joao. I was probably better off for having no preparation at all for it. My questions
flowed freely and conversationally. Joao started telling me how much
money he'd saved the City of New York. Helping the indigent, clear-
ing out the ER, curing the hypochondriachal and otherwise. We
started adding it all up. Eight thousand, twenty thousand, forty-
seven thousand, a hundred and thirty-three thousand. The number
growing with each retelling. I took a few notes. I began to be a little
bit glad that Maisie was late. My nervous system alive with my big
chance, to get something in the *New Yorker*, to get on with that part
of my life, to be a writer after all. So that, actually, after a little while
with Joao, whose English seemed strung together with oddly jagged
phrases, as if he were composing ransom notes from words cut out
of the newspaper, I found myself hardly sensing at all. Or rather, I
didn't find myself. Forget "stop." Forget "go back." Forget "gently."
I was swept up in the possibilities that my new gap-toothed friend
was giving me. Not that he treated me as a friend. Plainly he

would rather have been interviewed by Philip. Immigrant on the economic and cultural margins or no, he still knew where the butter was. "I tell this to Philip?" "Philip writes what magazine, *New York* magazine?"

Joao finished his bourbon. None the worse for it. But he didn't want another, he had professional principles, work to do, Christmas Eve, slow night, but there would be stabbings coming into the hospital for sure, Christmas Eve people still hurt each other and themselves. Joao's words, he could get rhetorical as hell, when it came to his mission.

Philip asked if I could go back to the hospital with him. Joao said could Philip come back, he could show Philip too many things. Philip said he couldn't get away, the party, people coming, but I could be his eyes and ears. In the end, with an averted gaze, Joao accepted me as Philip's eyes and ears. Some old disc from England of Noel Coward and Gertrude Lawrence was on the phonograph now. Philip had been, in a patch of moonlighting, some travel magazine's record critic for awhile and there were hundreds of records stacked in his closet, from which he'd plucked these reedy, ghostly voices, their sophistication weathered by the scratchy low fidelity. The music and the bourbon must have kicked in more or less at once on Joao, who before we left grabbed Philip around both arms the way he'd once laid hands on me at Saint Vincent's and began dancing him around the floor, by way of saying thank you for having him come here, no one could ask him for Christmas because he was far from Brazil, except Philip, who was his friend who did and now there would be this story and everyone will see how much money he saves New York which is very broke and so they will give him a green card. Philip backed off Joao's embrace as gingerly as he could. He was anyway as averse to dancing as I was.

Joao and I were tramping down the stairs just as Bobby climbed them. I imagined I saw something alike between the two, a slyness, or maybe just their size, or was it an elfin sensitivity that I'd become familiar with in Bobby but hadn't expected to see soon again. I introduced them. They didn't shake hands. We stood there a moment, Bobby taking off his woolen gloves.

"Seen Maisie?"

"No. Where are you going?"

"Over to Saint Vincent's. Do this story. On this guy."

"Great. Great."

Joao raising a hand.

The three of us standing there another moment with nothing to say.

"If Maisie shows up, would you tell her I'll be back?"

"I will."

Bobby raised his hand like Joao's and we went out.

'Twas Christmas in the Pest House. Bobby's favorite cartoon. But I didn't attach a vivid clarity to the memory until we got to the Saint Vincent's emergency. Just like Criminal Court AP-5, a good enough example of life's ongoingness. Something also about what purgatory must be about, in particular contrast to the cultivated warmth of Philip's apartment.

But here did they not save lives?

Indeed a slow night. Only half the plastic chairs filled. No wait to get a nurse to sign you up. It was Joao's practice to sign in with some ailment or other, then leave before his name was called. This, he felt, technically kept him from getting kicked out, kept the security guards off his case anyway. But it was all with a wink and a nod. Only the most newbie of the nurses didn't know who he was. The cute henna'd Puerto Rican girl on duty Christmas Eve seemed to like having him around.

Joao turned out to have a bit of regularized technique. The way he'd been with me a couple weeks before was how he behaved with everyone else. He would park himself a plastic chair or two away from a waiting patient and when things got slow strike up a conversation. This and that, the wait, the comparative charms of New York's different emergency rooms, the weather. Then, slowly coming around to it, he asked his questions, did his diagnosis, offered his services. People were always skeptical, but whether they chased him off or accepted him seemed to depend on a mysterious congeries of factors, impatience, poverty, trust or mistrust of who or what, who did you mistrust more. Also, a quality of receptivity? A slow night in the ER was even slower for Joao, because the less time people had to wait the less likely they were to put themselves in his hands. It occurred to me while we were waiting that I might ambush a resident and query him about Hodgkin's disease, the New Yorker having had nothing on its shelves, why not kill two birds? But Joao soon engaged a confused old woman in conversation. She thought she was back in Poland. She was a child and her hand had a booboo and where was her mother on Christmas? Or maybe I had some of this wrong, the woman's fuzzy chin tucked into the folds of her neck and her voice had a shrill, leaking air quality that made it difficult to follow what was already not very logical thought. But her hand plainly had been burned, from scalding water or maybe some pot she'd been cooking with, the entire back of it was red and blistering. I found it difficult to imagine what Joao could do for this woman. I even became fearful he was going to massage her arm or something equally ineffectual and tell her to go home and she'd leave and not get the care she needed and then what would our story be, non-medical malpractice by a scrawny *poseur*? Or would the story be conspiracy by an Assistant D.A. to promote unlawful professional practices? Joao's black eyes took her in, neither friendly nor unfriendly, not intense nor mild, more the seen-it-all eyes of the scientist I'd seen the other week. But when he took her hand it was as if she were a princess, he let her fat fingers drape over his like ripe fruit, and he kissed it. "You have beautiful hands," he said.

The woman's flesh-narrowed eyes widened. "I love you too."

Joao stood up. "Wait for help. You understand?"

"Wait for help," she repeated, and kissed her hand herself.

We left. I didn't ask.

So did I have here the Angel of Saint Vincent's or the Lothario of Saint Vincent's? He was keeping his secrets to himself now, his small, slightly rodential features in a kind of studied equipoise, as if his display of virtuosity was self-evident.

I resolved to go back when he wasn't around and ask everybody a ton of questions.

Then as we walked east, cold raindrops began to fall, fat and random, and as the little bullets of moisture began to bat us, I felt a subtle wave of elation, breathing in the cold rain, appraising my fresh success at being in the world but not of it. Gurdjieff said the worst position for a man was to be between two stools, but for the moment I was loving precisely this bifurcation, like a giant spreading his legs far apart, one foot in one world and one in another, each world serving as ballast, as collateral, for my forays into the other. And if I could write a story about Saint Vincent's, could I not follow it up with stories about the D.A.'s office? I could quit my job, I could churn them out, I could be ironic about the city and funny and charming like Philip and write sentences that ran like fresh water. My mind was full of plans, to the degree I very nearly forgot Joao with his pride and mystery walking right beside me. Stop. Go back. People could pass their whole lives and not remember that there was someone walking beside them. Joao interrupted our shared silence by tendering me his calculation that he'd just saved the City of New York eighty or ninety dollars. His Christmas present to the city. Joao split off from me at Sixth and 12th. He was taking the train to Brooklyn. We said good night. He said he would call Philip to see when this story would be coming.

I went on to 13th Street. Four o'clock or thereabouts. No muggers in sight. A car alarm somewhere. The rain abating. When you sense the nerves and sinews of your arms and legs more intensely, you feel something like you're walking on air. Not the musical comedy metaphor but something more specific and cognizable, as though your arms are propelling you along and you don't really need the ground as much as you thought. Or perhaps a closer metaphor would be the sense of swimming through air. I buzzed Philip's and was buzzed in. I climbed the stairs trying out various subvocalized formulations of how I should thank him. Stop. Go back. No words. I remembered "no words" just before I got to the door, then remembered that "no words" were already words. On and on. Nice try.

Coward and Lawrence had given way to Fred Astaire and Ginger Rogers on Philip's phonograph. Oh Rio, Rio by the sea, oh. Flying down to Rio where there's rhythm and rhyme. I heard it already in the hall, a siren song all the more seductive for being muffled and faint. Philip held the door open for me. I walked in and there were Joe and Maisie dancing cheek-to-cheek. Bobby was playing Clue and ignoring them. Maisie didn't even look my way. For a big man Joe was graceful on his feet and Maisie loved being twirled.

CHAPTER 16

AND SO. AND SO. Really, is there more to be said about it?

*

Though one thing that might be said is that Maisie's glands were not swollen. She'd simply been afraid.

*

Let us turn our attention to jollier things, shall we?

*

Current events. There's a good one. Always on the list, when a change of topic is desired. The late seventies, what a wonderful epoch, so much going on.

Disco whip inflation now Jimmy Carter Vegas Pintos homicides galore Abe Beame Church Commission Star Wars the movie not the missile defense recession stagflation peace.

All these came and went while we minded our own business. Really, we didn't care. Made a few jokes. Joe flew a flag on Earth Day. The world would always be there, one thing or the other. Gurdjieff's group in Russia worked right through the Revolution, moving from here to there, staying a half-step ahead of history.

*

An alternative formulation of why people came to the group. It had nothing to do with self-understanding. It had nothing to do with existential doubt. It may have had something to do with the temper of the times, what was permitted and what was still denied, the teetering of established frameworks, but mostly it had to do with power.

A boy grows with all kinds of dreams of taking on the world. He gets to a certain age and it looks like it's not going to happen. The socioeconomic cultural historical psychological biological "realities" begin to settle in. He's looking much smaller than his dreams. Someone holds a hand out. "Shut your eyes and come this way. All your difficulties will be removed." The boy follows, hoping to recoup, hoping to get it all after all.

The Faustian bargain all over again?

*

But then, that might have been only one boy's story.

*

My unhappy childhood, my father going away, my mother in disarray.

The point was, to get it out there so you could get past it. Treat it tenderly, so that you could get past it.

Kissing our hurt wings, so that each bird could fly.

*

Or, on some other occasion, less politely put: "One more unhappy childhood. Big fucking deal."

*

Bobby asked Joe once, years before, "Are you asking us to give up our minds, our conscious minds, the only ones we're aware of?"

"You'll have to tell me."

"I think you are. And if you are . . . don't our conscious minds . . . aren't they our moral factor, our conscience? . . ."

"Your superego."

""My conscience. Which, if I give it up . . . I mean, that's not too responsible."

"Then don't give it up, if you don't want to."

"That's what the Germans did, with Hitler, gave up their rational minds, because Hitler said there was something deeper."

"The Germans were crazy."

"But . . . aren't we a little like that?"

"Do you think I'm Hitler?"

"I don't know who you are."

"That's honest, at least."

"On the other hand, I think, what if it's the only way to get from here to there? Getting rid of all the baggage. Sooner a camel passes through the eye of a needle . . ."

"Than?"

"A lot of American Tourister?"

"Guess you'll just have to leave your luggage in the hands of someone you trust. Use your conscious mind to try to determine if there's someone you can entrust your precious baggage to."

"I do . . ."

"And?"

"I don't think my conscious mind can ever reach a conclusion."

"I don't think so either."

"But can it give me hints?"

"Can it?"

"I think so."

"And if you let your unconscious instincts percolate through . . ."

"That isn't fair."

"Isn't it? Doesn't your conscious mind tell you it's necessary?"

"My conscious mind doesn't tell me anything for sure."

"It can't."

"I don't know if I can trust you."

"Then suffer."

One of a thousand snippets of inquiry, that ended with Joe's shrug.

*

Who was Joe? Kike from Bensonhurst. Pratt. Head of the whole design department, didn't that mean something? In his field, then, a bit of a success. Skidmore Owings for awhile. The big time, in his telling of it, projects worth hundreds of millions. Which he would recall as if to certify his worth in the world, so that people wouldn't think he had a quarrel with it based on failure or resentment. Then India. Then the Old Painter. Then cancer. A divorce in there somewhere. What would the ex say? That he was angry, of course, that he'd gone off some deep end. Had the ex been a part of the Old Painter's group? Probably. I didn't know.

Was Joe kind? Perhaps. Funny? Perhaps. Shrewd? Perhaps.

Perhaps perhaps perhaps.

More than most Joe defeated the urge of the Other to catalog and define, to place people in a box of their characteristics. Long live the fluidity of man!

Was he enlightened, however much he trashed the word?

Perhaps.

One step up the ladder from the rest of us?

Perhaps.

Deluded and sicko and dogmatic and small-minded and good with a slide rule but in the end without humanity?

Perhaps.

He was "on" all the time. That was the claim, and even what it seemed.

That he'd been "on" so long, it was actually natural now. What he'd discovered, what he'd changed into, was more "him" than anything he'd been before.

This seemed, generally, true. There was something very specific about Joe, even when you subtracted the teacher part.

Don't act out of negative emotions, he'd say, but then he'd act out whatever he seemed to want to act out and it wouldn't be "negative."

Or was it "negative" but it didn't matter because he was in a different place from us, with different rules, or no rules at all?

Playing with words? Hypocrisy?

Or lessons in the suppleness of life.

Could we see how the two were different, his emotions and ours? Was he watching his more subtly? Even, playing games with them, luxuriating in them, feeling further emotions, of nostalgia, of fond distance, on account of his awareness of his emotions?

Mostly, Joe seemed kind of brave. Jaunty and brave, like an actor who's overcome stage fright.

*

The whole question of "help." The group seemed to be about "helping people." Joe was "helping" us, for which we paid him, but not, according to his occasional pronouncements, by way of an equal bargain, because the help he gave us couldn't be priced; rather, he asked to be paid, he said, because people valued something more if they had to pay for it; also it cost him money to run the group. Forty dollars a month per person. Cheap therapy, if that's what you thought it was. In turn Joe reminded us that most of us did little to help anybody else, for which we were not to blame because we were basically incapable of it. In this respect, masturbation was an apt enough metaphor, a wry, if cogent, example. We must clear our own minds before being able to see clearly the minds of others. And if we could see clearly the minds of others, would we know how to help them?

People in their confusion often wanted things that didn't help them.

But help them to do, or be, what, then?

Make a little more money get laid live life more intensely be healthy wealthy and wise? Jobs relationships parents bosses lovers the past the present the future sagging tits and migraines the nuts and bolts the stuff that therapists get paid for their meat and potatoes their bread and butter their clichés.

But what then, and who cared? When the person—as was the way of men?—was still dissatisfied?

Then and only then, the question might arise: were they suitable for the work?

Did they have a sincere desire to understand themselves?

Was that even the question?

Was that the one true help?

And which of us could provide it?

Joe?

Take nothing on faith.

No leaps of faith.

Was that possible?

*

Cheek-to-cheek they danced. He dipped her as though they were at a high school prom. Maisie who'd never been to such a prom, who'd gone to boarding schools all the way.

Why wouldn't she look at me? Of course she wouldn't look at me. She'd moved on, again.

And why shouldn't she, wasn't that a part of her magnificence?

What negative emotions did I feel? Let's catalog them.

Hatred. Bitterness. Envy. Anger. Fear. Humiliation. Shame.

Depression is anger, isn't depression anger?

And yet.

I also felt a numbing sadness, as though part of me had been washed out to sea.

Why had Maisie come to New York in the first place? Joe who'd had cancer too. Joe who it was said could help her.

Could I have helped her?

My gush of sentiment, my hauling up of ghosts, stirring her and us around, distractions, playing around, encouraging her own old ghosts.

I'd been hunting in the king's preserve all along.

CHAPTER 17

CHOPPING AWAY. CHOP CHOP. Chop chop chop chop chop chop chop chop chop chop chop chop. How many times can I say it? How many times could I think it or hear it? Chop, which doesn't really sound very much like what it represents, and even less so in my mind's watery reverberations. Where is the thudding essence, where is the variety, the thwacking groans, the aches, the claps, the flat bangs, the breathy stretches of the blade? Instead of saying "chop" why don't I simply listen to the blade? Why must everything be interpreted, the world put in place? Stop. Go back. My new Chinese cleaver, my Christmas present to myself, its handle bright with shellac, its blade branded with two pictographs, like chicken feet, genuine, irreducible, of which I have no comprehension.

The slab of it, the weight, the way it pounces on the scallions, like a big guy who is also fast. Christmas morning in the loft. I've come down at nine o'clock to do some prep for later in the day and I've brought my cleaver with me. Scallions then bok choy then Chinese broccoli then whatever else Bobby's stuffed into the fridge as if getting ready to feed the Union Army. I let the blade fall mostly on its own. I flick my wrist lightly, a priest dispensing holy water. It is odd, perhaps, that having "given up" possessions, having professed nonattachment, I've never been prouder of the few things I own. A cleaver, a working tool, something that bears infinite inspection, for its evolution, its stately history written in steel, its blood sport, its necessity.

I chop like a madman, feeling what I feel must be the bright breath of a sleepy Christmas morning, sun's out, frost cusping my precious clean panes, feeling nothing at all really but wondering why I feel so good, as now the bok choy falls in a heap. Buckets of bok choy. It has a crunch when it dies. It is white and green like a distant morning. Iceland. Greenland. Is Joe still sleeping? Does the loft smell faintly of his farts? I wish he'd come out and see my cleaver.

Back in his bedroom. A folding screen instead of a door. Is Maisie there? Stirring now. A bit of rustling back there, creaks of the floor. My neck tenses. I chop with self-conscious intensity. Too much. Phony? Go back.

When Joe comes out, it's in his terry robe of many colors. Gray eyes still narrow in sleep, he almost looks Chinese. Mongolian, anyway, Siberian. One of those Jews who went to Birobidzhan? Hair mussed. He stretches his arms out lazily, fists balled up, like a round, quickly drawn figure in a Zen cartoon, or a shmoo. Good morning. Hi. He throws the switch on the coffeepot, comes over to see what I'm doing. Stands in back of me as if to drive me nuts but I don't turn around. "Maisie's still asleep," he says, and there's nothing I can say to that.

"Am I chopping too loud?"

"No."

And then:

"You buy that?"

"This? Uh-huh."

"Nice."

Chop chop. Chop chop chop chop chop.

"Maisie's head . . . My head . . . Maisie's head . . . My head . . . You would've made a great executioner. Monsieur Danton, let Louie do it. He knows how these newfangled machines of decapitation work."

I grin nervously or is it smile grimly, or was it both? Both and all of it, but I do not turn. Too cool to turn around or glare or catch his glance.

"Maisie's head . . . my head . . . mom's head . . . dad's head . . . my head . . . Maisie's head . . ."

I continue to grin nervously or smile grimly, as I hear the tease in his voice. Not mean, nothing really mean, but certain, his singing delight, as if he were yelling "Gotcha!"

He pours himself a mug of coffee. I can see his Joseph robe out of the corner of my eye. The Little King, who like everybody else before breakfast looks ten years older.

"Want some?" Of the coffee.

"No thanks. I'll finish this first."

He pours his half-and-half, casts a glance at my working profile, his Santa Claus glint on full display. "Get it?" Joe asks me.

He wanders off as I say nothing and continue to chop. But get fucking what? Maisie's head? My father's head? My mother's head! This is precisely what I *do* get, yes I fucking get what I fucking get is precisely this ridiculous certainty, this simpleminded, paperback Freud on the cheap two-bit ignorant shit, this "one-way-or-another-I'm-me-so-I-must-be-right," this patronizing condescending self-righteous shit, but most of all this fucking "Get it?" grin. Get fucking what? Get laid, that's what. Jesus, the fatuity of it all.

And not even of it "all," not of Philip not of Bobby not of Maisie, but of Joe.

Maisie's head Joe's head, my father's head my mother's head.

Oh now that's real profound.

That's going to get me across the river assuming I even want to get across some fucking river or whatever's the metaphor du jour.

I chop. Chop chop chop chop chop chop chop chop chop chop. Maisie's head. Joe's head.

Well, Joe's head at least.

Does it lighten my load to chop off his head?

Does it lead to my delight?

In five minutes I'm exhausted. I pour myself a cup of coffee and sit.

Maisie's up now. Joe owns a second coat-of-many-colors, for his guests, and Maisie's wearing it now. It works wildly with her red hair, all but bleeds it out.

But she's cheerful enough.

"Hi . . . I should explain." Breathy, throaty morning voice.

"No need."

She takes me at my word. She's not one to go where she isn't wanted. Wary of traps, plays the world like a battlefield.

Or was that the learned behavior of the group? Was it any longer possible for me to figure out what was there before and what came with the new territory?

"My glands weren't swollen. Sorry. False alarm," she says.

"I knew it," I say, and leave it at that.

I am on to the Chinese broccoli now. Having the job to do steadies me. What did I even think of Maisie?

When I saw her this morning I felt a sort of silly shame, as if I knew I couldn't touch her but couldn't remember exactly why.

Maisie, you devil.

Maisie, you doll.

Wandering around the loft now. Both of them wandering around, I wasn't sure doing what, like two planets loosed from their orbits.

While I chop. Choppity-chop, the greater resistance of the Chinese broccoli to my blade. I chop harder. I will not stand for resistance. I take control. I do what is needed. I am I, after all.

My rage begins to overtake me, begins to lighten my load. I am so angry my face must redden and I feel lightheaded and for a moment I notice it is all without words. Or almost without words, words getting as sparse as signs in a desert.

Have I ever been so mad and it is all about nothing. I pity my mother, who fell apart. I pity my father, who was so weak to run away. But I do not pity myself because I have no pity for myself it's an empty well gone dry gone fishing forget myself now. Haunt my rage. Inhabit it, come to know it. And the pity like soft moss growing in the dark beneath.

I do not know how long it is and all my food is chopped. Neat pieces of equal size, meet for stir-fry, job well-done.

I wipe my cleaver dry with a paper towel then oil it with vegetable oil. Is this how? How can it not be "how," it's my cleaver, my blade, my instrument. Whose head should it chop off next? Any that I decide but why should I decide. My rage is too much fun. It lightens too much of my load.

And just think, milady, it was down there all along, mucking about in the basement, fouling up the plumbing. We'll take care of it now, we'll get it all set to rights, air the place out, good as new.

Yes? No? Yes and no?

I feel like crying, for pity, for my mother, for my father.

What have they got to do with any of this?

Not to blame, not to blame.

Are we really well past Freud, or any number of steps behind?

Or right on time?

All right on time.

No words.

Few words, anyway.

And yet, for a moment. I love words!

The hidden genius of humanity. Hiding in plain sight.

Yes? No? Yes and no?

I've never quite loved words before. Now that I'm giving them up.

A few seconds anyway, maybe more, maybe it's more now.

Rage, the cleansing genius.

In my peripheral vision Joe waddling around. Flicking on the lights of the Christmas tree. Their multicolored gleam, his multicolored robe.

Is color all right, after all?

Is the world all right, after all?

The shushing of the shower. The water tickling Maisie's back, bouncing off her flesh, her breasts, dripping her and stripping her. Down the drain with your sins, my love. We're all reborn. You too. So, fuhgeddaboudit.

Didn't I say that stupid thing to you one time?

Sing to me. Sing in the shower. I can't hear your voice but if you're singing I'll know that you are.

I put my vegetables in bowls and wax paper over the bowls and put the bowls in the fridge, my hands, my fingers, my arms, cool and calculated, no effort lost. Elegant I am. Necessary I am. Joe is pouring himself a second cup of coffee and asks again if I want some.

I sit with him. The coffee tastes of gold. The shower water ceases. She must be drying off but I do not think *she is drying off.* A medicine cabinet opens and shuts. The bathroom is actually quite far away, twenty feet or so. Joe looks like a tired Buddha today, rings under his eyes, dark and planetary, and slightly gory with his biblical, his faux-biblical robe.

For once I am not afraid of him. Why should I be afraid? Naked citizens of the world, unite.

Joe renders me with a bloodless stare. I feel strung from head to toe. I feel joyous.

"Breakthrough?" Joe asks.

In that neutral tone, that I always thought was conscious and contrived but now I guess he can't even help. When the situation calls for it, it just comes out.

Could it be that Joe plans nothing at all? That he just reacts?

I think I hear him say "Breakthrough?" again, but it echoes, he only says it once.

I don't know.

But I am giddy.

I am speechless.

I believe Joe is a great man. Joe must know something. I am his partner, sidekick, amigo. I am here. This is enough. Fuck Maisie who cares tell her to go get us some more half-and-half. Which I sort of think and which when she comes out of the shower he actually does, he says, Maisie would you go get us some half-and-half?

Oh I am up on the world today.

But Maisie says she has a headache and she needs to lie down. She looks washed and pale. I hardly recognize her.

I sit for a while with Joe.

Everything subsides. Whatever "everything" was.

I leave around eleven. Joe's going to watch the football and I've got to get my things together for the week. My changes of clothes, my money, my candy, toothbrush, whatever more. Be prepared.

Motto of melancholy and springtime.

I walk to the train at Broadway-Lafayette. On the way uptown my car is laced with people going to church. I feel engaged. I feel grand. Who cares how I feel? It's not who you know but what you know but who you know, or is it? A big guy with his legs sprawled in the aisle of the train. Jews in their paperbacks. Guys off work, guys who worked Christmas Eve. Somewhere after 34th Street the train stops dead and the lights go off. The gloaming of the emergency power. All our faces in shadow. The engine cuts out. People breathe, people mind their own business, those who were hanging from straps still clutch them, as if they don't want to lose what they've got if the train starts again, or they don't want to be caught off guard. Guys sleeping with their noses in the *Daily News*. Headline at an angle about the Pope in Rome and midnight mass. Rustling among the pigtailed girls, the boys in suits, their mamas quick to hush. Suddenly all voices can be heard. There are few of them. People embarrassed to speak, to be known. The darkness, the shadows, the strange breaths. Who *are* all these people?

Why are we together? And it occurs to me, too, are we going to stay together? Have we always been and will we always be?

Who *says* this train's going to move?

Oh *sure*, it'll move. But when? After forever?

Because this is starting to feel like forever.

We all know that time can slow but did we know that it could slow among strangers underground in the dark and electric silence?

Come now, come now, calm down, take a breath no don't take a breath hold your breath didn't Joe say once if too much starts coming up just hold your breath and that will stop it all?

I hold my breath. It stops nothing. I hold my breath again. I am afraid of these angel children. I am afraid of the guy's sprawled legs. I am afraid of the crinkling newspapers and the silence and the cool that's entering the car because the engine's off, the noise is off, the heat is off, everything off. Is this what Joe calls a "breakthrough," is this what a "breakthrough" is? I'm going to die down here. I am going to die, anyway and sometime, but it seems it's going to be here. I'll go crazy I'll jump out on the tracks. Get me out of here. Claustrofucking-phobia a disorder in the *DSM*. I'll jump on the third rail. What have I gotten myself into?

It's this work, it's this exercise, it's this shutting these words out of my head and this sensing everything, how can I be sensing everything? I don't want to sense everything, I don't want to sense this car, this dark, this stuff, these breathing people, I am a freak, I've made a mistake, go back, no don't go back going back is what Joe says to do going back is part of it too, no, go forward, go forward, I don't want to understand myself and never did, it's alienated me from everybody turned me into a freak who will find me now who will penetrate who will ever know who will come get me. I am alone, and stuck down here. I am afraid.

CHAPTER 18

GO FORWARD, GO FORWARD. Which is what we eventually do, to the next station.

At the next station I got out and walked.

And as I walked did I "think" or did I think?

What is thought? What is hallucination? Is thought hallucination? Is "thought" hallucination?

I do not want to go crazy. I do not want to lose control. If I go crazy and lose control won't I kill myself, won't I do some powerful thing?

*

Joe said don't use drugs, drugs are hallucination, drugs are distraction, from what is.

And drugs use up finer energy and when the drugs wear off it's gone.

And you haven't earned anything.

But at the moment, as I walk, the breeze from the river slapping my face awake, I think of things quite the other way: at least with drugs you'd know it would be over, you'd know it's not forever. You could tell yourself and wait it out.

But this? This, what, this terror? Which is. Which is what it is. Is without end, because what will end it?

Kill yourself. Kill yourself, that'll kill it, or will it?

One more dismal idea. Think you can escape just by death?

Hamlet come alive, at last.

Sententious phrases galore, come alive, at last.

Or at least I see what they were pointing their crabby arthritic fingers at.

Fear.

So there's something about what Joe's about, after all, and maybe it's subtle and fine and gentle in the end but for the moment it's bigger than a bomb. Blow me up anyway, blow up my world.

I feel small and stupid.

How dare I . . . what? Step clumsily on the hem of it all? Curse, be casual, ignore, pretend to a million false truths?

I am afraid enough of death and if there's more than death . . .

Who can stand this? Who is man enough?

And so have I not played a neat game of approach-avoidance?

It's an old game for me, but let's say, for argument's sake, that's true of us all, monkeys running at the fire, monkeys touching it or just feeling the heat, monkeys running away.

I pretend to myself I'm Birdman, I'm a venturer a seeker-after-something a careener through life on the lookout for what it's about, but if I get the smallest hint of what it's about I am so struck with awe and speechless I run I cry surrender make excuses regroup reconsider reconnoiter reinterpret every pledge and every word, every gesture.

I like reading about things at my house in my comfy chair in front of my comfy fire if I even had a fire. Armchair general, dreaming of battles that are far enough away. Yes or no? Me or not me?

Continue, please.

Continue.

*

Maybe later I won't be so afraid. Later, when I'm again far enough away, or when I'm nestled anyway in the softness of Joe's voice, when others will be there to cheer or back up, there for each other or anyway stuck together, thirty birds on a journey to where.

*

It's ignoble to be between two stools. It makes you two-faced. But I'm comfortable that way, admit it. To the world, I say one thing. To this other world, another.

*

I buy a paper at the newsstand at 86th Street. I continue to my apartment. I get my things together for the event. I watch a little of the football. The Jets are getting pasted.

By the second half my fear has retreated.

CHAPTER 19

BOBBY AND I SAW her with the same eyes that night, Maisie sitting cross-legged on the floor, hunched a little forward, between Laura and Joe, her impertinent hair like her entire biography saying she might be anywhere tomorrow. Her half-eaten meal between her legs, that Bobby had prepared, his secret gift to her, still close to her when he was not. Maisie didn't *act* like she was a blessing to wherever she happened to be, but either of us might have seen her that way. The only difference being that I saw Bobby looking as well, and he didn't see me. That's how I knew, or thought I knew, that for once I was the man and he was the boy. The night of Christmas, after both of us had looked at Maisie, Bobby and I went out to find some girls.

My idea entirely, like taking Junior to a whore, buck him up, back in the saddle. Both of us having been left. My gesture of friendship. For once, something I could do. And was it, as well, proof to myself of my own immunity? I am not attached to Maisie, I let

Maisie roll off me, she can get Hodgkin's disease Stage 112 and die or so I tell myself and wonder why. The meeting after dinner lasted until almost ten. Talking about the "event," prepping for the "event," Joe's pep talk, follow your aim, hold your question, "Damn the torpedoes! Full speed ahead!"

Bobby looked so gloomy. Dead goldfish look, out on the street, on Broadway. Come on, let's do it. He didn't really know what I was talking about, the few girls in Bobby's life having either come to him or been there. Bobby wasn't a hunter, but it was my gesture to act as if he might be or anyway wouldn't it be fun for once, cheerful anyway, new way to kill a little time. Bobby when are we gonna cut the gloom shit out? What happened to the principle of nonattachment? Let it come and let it go. Don't censor but don't believe. Plenty of mermaids in the sea, just look at me, I didn't say; nor any of the rest of it. But I behaved as if it were so, and maybe to humor me he tried, with a skeptic's chilled bemusement, to go along. "It's pretty late."

"Who cares?"

"It's Christmas."

"Lonely hearts."

"I didn't know bars were open on Christmas." The kind of thing that Bobby wouldn't know.

Roget's on Broadway in the eighties might as well have been closed. The bartender looked at us every several minutes with a lingering purposefulness, as if maybe we'd leave and he could close up. I bought Bobby a drink and felt the lofty trajectory of my patronization despite the fact there wasn't a woman in sight. Bobby picked at the label of his beer. The place smelled of leftover cold cuts, wafted from a dreamtime steam table. I wondered with half-formed words how I had got to this position, where I could fall in love one day and say fuck her the next. Had I not been a sensitive child? Felt all the stings of rejection. Yet here I was, giving manly advice on John Suckling's subject; a kind of suspect miracle. And Bobby who was ahead of me in pretty much everything else was stuck.

Or was he?

Had I not become, on further reflection, rather a cold insensitive anesthetized bastard?

Go back. Gently. Fuck "further reflection," and furthermore "reflection."

Sense, look, listen.

But why bother if it turns us into automatons?

It doesn't turn us into automatons, it doesn't turn us *into* anything, it turns us *towards* . . . what?

How say it?

Bobby and I not saying any of this, but all of it alive between us, inchoate, at issue.

All the venerable travails of love, the doubt, the longing, the misery of absence, the aspiration and striving and proving, redirected away from breast and womb, warm blood and earthy lies, towards . . . dot dot dot again.

No, no. No, no, that's wrong. That's the propaganda. That's the ideal. In truth, I'm between two stools. I don't love anything now. I don't know what to love. Have I begun to love myself?

Joe? Love Joe? I don't love Joe. I don't "love" Joe. Does Bobby love Joe? Does Bobby "love" Joe?

We're so miserably lost.

Except that Bobby "loves" Maisie. What a throwback. What a disaster. How could Bobby feel so much for Maisie, that he sits here and peels his beer label like a boy? Maisie who must have been for him an image, a symbol, a hint, an embodiment but of what?

Or that other word they use, incarnation. Fuck incarnation. Fuck it all. Bobby come back. Stop. Sense. Look.

Is Bobby advanced or is he fallen by the road? All a race after all.

What a bore, to race through life. What a chore. A little of this, a little of that. A thousand "I's," a thousand Bobbies. But which one do we have here in Roget's on Christmas night? The one that loves Maisie or "loves" Maisie, that's mournful and alive with hate for Joe for taking her?

"Bobby, are you," I ask. "Bobby are you mad at him?"

He shrugs as would be expected and his thumb nubs at the remains of his label.

Don't tell me how life should be, don't tell me how to be. He seems to be saying?

Yes Bobby I was wrong about girls tonight, no lonely hearts, I say, more or less.

Close to him, rubbing shoulders with him. His narrow shoulders, his slender arms. Mine slender but not as slender as his.

"It doesn't matter at all," he says.

But it does, I almost say.

Bobby says, "If I was mad at Joe for being with Maisie wouldn't I be mad at you as well?"

"I guess you would."

"But I'm not," he says, "I'm not, I never was. And not because I 'let go' any feelings."

"Why, then?"

"Who knows."

"Girls are better at this than we are," I say.

And by "this" I think he'll know what I mean but maybe he won't. Bobby shrugs. Good enough. Warm-blooded anyway.

The way of the sly man, sitting in bars, a few others have passed in and out or lingered by now, and now a girl I met in here a couple months ago from South Dakota walks in.

How rude of me not to make up her name. Barbara.

Her name is Barbara. Barb, they say in Sioux Falls.

So Barb, this is my friend Bobby. Buy Barb a beer. Too cold to go back to South Dakota or nobody to go back to. A little unclear with Barb. Her heavy frame, her sluggish good nature.

She may weigh twenty pounds more than Bobby.

She enters into our conversation, the one that we weren't really having.

What'd you do today and how've you been and is it starting to snow, what a trip it would be if it snowed. Barb like a lone lamppost on a block. She remembers me well, she's happy to see me, but now I have to do the good-guy-horseshit-thing-of-the-year, win that award for once I've got to pass Barb along to Bobby so I do the ob-vious things, I praise Bobby to considerable heights, I mention the *New Yorker*, did she see his Mister All Electric Kitchen, if she didn't (which she didn't and she too, *vox populi*, conflates the *New Yorker* with *New York*), she really must. I do not mention the group, I do not mention anything weird, we are in the world now and we play the world's games as well as anybody.

Bobby for his part has little to say, but his smile is strawberry jam. He was in South Dakota once. There's that. Mount Rushmore. He draws Mount Rushmore on a napkin. Our presidents funny, cockeyed, insane, their noses and hair too pointed and their eyes too close. Barb isn't quite amused though she looks like she thinks she ought to be. She seems a little afraid that Bobby might be the type to blow Mount Rushmore up. Wrong vibrations. Try again. Bobby as prospective bourgeois, steady job, praise from the top. Bobby as well-connected, Shaker Heights and all the rest of it. Bobby as poor slob on Christmas whose girl went away. Careful with mentioning the girl. Careful, careful, careful. But Bobby does it anyway because he doesn't know what to do. Our little naif, our shy, cunning Bobby. Mentioning Maisie was no good at all, I'd begun observing Barb's light mustache damp with beer and figured Bobby had too, things were not going well for Mister Fix-up, time for Plan B, plead illness upset stomach go home have to call Europe in the morning or maybe Kuala Lumpur all of it or some of it I forget which exactly but anyway I left them, rather abruptly. How cavalier, how dashing, how second-rate stud. As if the last thing to be done was whisper in Bobby's ear, *for me, Bobby, for me.*

But I didn't whisper that. I said to Barbara that Bobby might draw her on a napkin and one day it would be worth a mint, I said good night, left a well-calculated tip, and left.

On Broadway I found the phone booths calling out to me, singing to me like the Lorelei, streetwalkers one to a block, and what they were singing was BUtterfield 8.

No Maisie don't tempt me don't trick me again I walk up Broadway I'll not be detained not drop a dime in a phone when you won't be there anyway I know where you are.

Yet I'm shaken to think that I would even like to call her up. What a liar I am, what layers of self-deception, all that posing with Bobby. What a laugh, what a fake. And oddly or is it simply the way things always are, glorious in their banality, between men and women, between friendship and love: I know it for certain now, I like Bobby better than I like Maisie. As Marcel said of Albertine, all this and she wasn't even my type.

I do not dial 2-8-8. I go home and one way or another manage to notice on my hollow core door desk where I've scarcely sat for years my notes about Joao. For sure to spite them both, Maisie and Joe, to show them my dust and that I'm still alive, in an hour I sketch a story about the Angel of Saint Vincent's. It's full of blanks and strained and I have no magic to hide the lonesome "we" that every Talk story still in 1978 requires, but it's a start and when I'm done I want less to call BUtterfield 8.

Bobby phoned me around one when I was already in bed. He was home and he was alone. The gory details, just a few. Mildly apologetic. He'd drawn her on another napkin. She'd looked at herself, perplexed. Never mind the jaw too square the nose too long the eyes too beady . . . was that a mustache? Barb said that she too wasn't feeling well. Good Samaritan, good night. With the fewness of his words, Bobby sounded as if maybe he blamed me, for making a fool of him, or wasting his time.

CHAPTER 20

OUR SILENCE.

We did not talk about the group with others. It wasn't in any of our biographies.

Unless someone asked, or sensed something, from the *Bird Guide* or Philip's Talk stories or the person's prior experience with Ichaza or Castaneda or somebody.

Girlfriends and boyfriends inevitably found out, and often they wound up coming to meetings.

Later they would throw off the girlfriend or boyfriend who brought them and then they would stay or not, or the girlfriend or boyfriend who brought them would stay or not.

You never knew. Who would stick, who would go.

There was something erotic about it all, or something that started as erotic.

The circle. The quiet lack of inhibition.

The poetry of love.

The bright paint on the window frames of Joe's apartment.
The roses on their shelves, under their lights.

*

Our morality.
Once on a Tuesday evening:
Philip: Is morality conditioning?
Joe: Yes.
Philip: But do we need morality?
Joe: If people wised up, they wouldn't need it.
Philip: Ah.
Joe: In the meantime, that's why we've got cops.

*

People struggling to believe.

*

Whatever it is, struggling to believe.

*

Not *believing*. Believing would be different, believing would be like a machine without friction. Struggling to believe.

*

The "event."

We'll be spiffing up the place. Painting the window frames, sanding the floors, painting the old tin ceiling. Making a nice little home for whatever it is in a loft on the tenth floor. For Joe. Let's be specific. A nice little home for Joe. *Mi casa, su casa.* Why not? Didn't the village always support the parson? Respect for wisdom, even in New York in 1978. Respect for ourselves, Joe would say. Our home. Most hours of the day, somebody coming or going. The once-and-future clubhouse; workshop, too, carpenters, making tables, Jesus wannabes. What a vision. What an alternative. Build a workshop in yourselves, build a clubhouse in yourselves. The sort of things that Joe would say, we wouldn't even have to hear them, I wouldn't even have to hear them. Build a small place in yourselves, quiet and beautiful, where you can hear running water, and if the rest gets done, so much the better. Somewhere in the world, one place or the other, people have always done this work of cultivation. "We." "I." Whoever. The "event." On the eve of it Joe gives an example of an aim: "I/we/you will live or die trying." Tomorrow it starts.

CHAPTER 21

SEVERAL OF US SIT across a patch of the floor like oil derricks in a desert, fiefdoms of enterprise, going about our business with a seeming perpetual automatism. We are assigned to sanding the floor. Years of wax and grime and urethane clog its pores and encrust it with a hardened atmosphere of discoloration, as if it were wearing a petrified coat of smog. I see this theoretically, with my mind's eye that I must never trust but that operates nonetheless, guessing, judging, and criticizing. I have not yet seen what the boards will look like when they're bare. Even to say "boards" would be a stretch, since my eyes work on one board only, one portion of one board, the part of it where it meets the next board in line like a passenger car in a train, my universe, my country, home to all my history and efforts, a section of the unredeemed world two inches wide and ten inches long, give or take the occasional incursions into neighboring territory by accident, the scuffs and scratches on adjacent boards as if they've suffered collateral damage. By ten o'clock my mind is imprinted with a new language, in which "60" and "80" and "100" and "150" all have utilitarian meaning, the language of sandpaper. My chosen sanding block rests in my hand, small and rectangular, like a bar of soap you might get in a not overly generous hotel. Number sixty sandpaper is wrapped around it. I've not come even close to using an eighty yet. Coarse, that's my speed, I've a long way to go, even on this tiniest patch of board, to get to medium coarse. I sand with many light strokes. Infinitesimal dust rises and clings to my sandpaper and fingers. I do not overdo it. I have a long way to go, I tell myself with words then banish the words, in the proverbial manner of closing the barn door after all sorts of creatures have fled.

I shift my legs. I am stiff from the waist down. I half-recline like a Jew at Passover but in this position I find too little weight in back of my arm. The sanding block brushes over the board like a whisper. I shift again. My ass hates the floor. My flat, skinny ass that's already had enough of this. Why doesn't he assign the fat-assed people to sand the floor? Look at Laura, she could sand all day. Perfectly balanced on her two majestic cheeks, the natural Buddha of floors. Go back. Slow down. Sand. The muscle in my forearm feels like a burnt coil. I relax my fingers on the block. I inspect the sandpaper to see if it's still got grist. With the side of my hand I plow the dust away from the board. I do this too often, I decide, I'm like a windshield wiper when it's barely raining. Who decides? Why decide? Go back. Look at the floor, look at my board. Its grain is like a hundred streams. It is perhaps a shade lighter than when I began, perhaps a shade lighter than the boards that adjoin it. It makes a mottled appearance, some regions of it lighter, others, gullies and ravines, darker and less explained. The whole still glows dully with old wax. My knees ache too. It is ten o'clock. I've taken my watch off but I steal a glance at Joe's forearm as he trundles by

Jeffrey Lewis

on one of his trips. He's wearing a short-sleeve shirt as usual. The stainless steel watchband snakes and glints on his thick forearm. The blond hairs of his forearm make a prairie. Where's he going? Who cares? Go back.

I take a break. I sit in Joe's captain's chair, my hands on the armrests, symmetrical and loose. All around me the others sand and paint and hammer. As busy as little bees, though their affect looks more like the Stepford wives, pushing carts with slow stares. Oh don't ask why. Oh don't ask why. I still love Lotte Lenya. The no bullshit cruelty of Brecht. What would the wily old kraut commie make of this? Go back. But I don't go back. One thing to another, Brecht to Germans to Jews, their toothbrushes cleaning the sidewalks of Berlin or was it Vienna? What an idea that one was. Teach the people of the book a thing or two about manual labor. The virtues of work, work makes free. Are we Nazis now? Are we following a Nazi path, is my sanding block so different from the toothbrush? Look. Listen. Sense. Who? Me or them? Go back. The Jews were being humiliated and we are not being humiliated. Or are we? The Jews were not free to go and we are. Or aren't we? We are, I am! The world with its lessons. Could the Jews in servitude have learned a lesson of freedom? Maybe they did, maybe some did. You can learn anything from anybody but that doesn't make everything the same. Joe is not some sitcom guard and we are not Stalag 17, nor even with my bomber jacket do I make William Holden. How'd I get on this? Who cares. My break's gone on too long. I sit in Joe's chair and daydream. It doesn't matter if I work or rest, everywhere I daydream. Hopelessness is all.

I go back to sanding. This is only the first day, the first morning of the first day. I work a little while, then take another break. I am falling in love with breaks. Why not, no one's watching. What a

172

child. I long to go out. I long to go to the store, to buy more sand-paper. I change my sandpaper as often as I can. But still I have enough. When can I go outside, breathe the cool air, go to the store? And it occurs to me as well: why don't we go rent a sander? He wants the floor sanded, rent a sander. I long to go to the store to rent a sander.

No. Don't. Sense. Sand. My tired arm, my flat ass. The board as resistant as a stiff-necked Jew, as me myself and I. We are both encrusted, hardened, I see the comparison now, vividly, with pathos.

How could I have accumulated so much crud in thirty-two years?

It occurs to me this could be the same amount of time that's passed since the board's been sanded. What if it's been precisely thirty-two years, eight months, how many days, twenty-five days?

Not too bloody likely, but still.

Go back. Sense a *little bit*, anyway.

Yes I do. I sense my hand. I listen to the sibilant scratching of the paper against the floor. It's like a woman doing her nails. We'll never sand the whole floor like this.

To recapture the attention of my eyes or maybe out of boredom I look around. Maisie in jeans and a loose flannel shirt, cross-legged and shapeless, sorting papers out of a cardboard box, her red hair her emblem, like words that need never be said but if they could talk would say . . . what? Yes they would say "what," they would say "what" and then be still and intent and defiant, but right now she's not defiant, she's learning, she's young, or that's what it looks like anyway, she looks like a plant in the ground. And Philip and Joe washing windows, like a tag team, a comic duo, the sunshine boys as window washers, griping in silence, their lips not moving, Philip on one window, Joe the next, Joe's long arms, longer than mine, reaching up to the top window like Lamarque's giraffe to the top branches. Neither of them looking like they quite believe, having the postures of hypothesis and hope, their eyes, their hands, the glinting windows, all in mazy motion as if in Xanadu did Kubla Khan something or other decree, or in this case Kubla Kahn. Joe shaking his wrist, shaking his watchband, here and there the Little King the Little Kahn. A few words to Laura that I cannot hear, a few words to Ty, who's sanding too. I am doing a census now. I am checking everybody out, or at least those at this end of the loft, those this side of the galley, but the galley blocks my view of the rest. Joe bustles out of sight, towards the band saw. As he departs he leaves a wake, a fading contrail of attracted attention, a kind of evanescent evidence. Was he sensing? What was he sensing? The force of his wake, his one ball, his vitality. For a moment I like it. I like being part of a chance.

And Bobby in the galley, cooking alone. I long to move up. If I can't go to the store, at least I could be there. Like prisoners in the camps, again, hoping for minor improvements to their fates. As if everything depended on minor improvements, minor improvements like signs, or like moves on a chessboard, proof the game's still being played. You can leave! I chide myself, then chide myself for chiding myself, then chide myself for chiding myself about chiding myself. You can walk out anytime! There's that. Just test it. Go!

But if I went, what would I do with these friends I've made, these comrades of a long march? Really, I've gotten used to them. A world supplied. A world other than the one that is no more than it is, concrete image of itself, fetishized, commercial, world of indifferent betrayal. Something tender is here, or personal anyway.

Joe yells "Stop!" I hear the word penetrating my dream, I can almost see its force, a missile crashing down through my fantasy's atmosphere. Everyone holds whatever position they were in. My hand is tight, my neck muscles tense, my mouth hard and set. Flecks of dust on my fingers.

"Does anyone have anything they want to talk about?"

I steal a glance around. My neck gets tenser as my eyes move. Bobby with a spatula in the air, as if he were conducting an orchestra. Maisie hunched over, almost doubled up. Philip touching the connecting piece of his glasses, professorial, unsurprised, even relaxed. Is it possible he was really relaxed when Joe yelled "Stop"? Of course it is. There are things undreamt of in my philosophy, but I am beginning to dream them now.

Maybe I am, could it be that I am?

The only one with anything to say is hatchet-faced Phyl, previously notable for having been picked up for prostitution on the Bowery, to wit a French for twenty dollars U.S. currency said the officer, while Phyl told the group it was certainly her first time and only on account of an unexpected cash crunch, terrible luck; which I said nothing about but found hard to believe because with the efficiency of the New York vice squad as I knew it to be you'd have to have given eight or ten thousand blow jobs before the odds of a bust went against you. But anyway Phyl who I can't look at now without thinking of what a wide and tolerant assemblage we are, writers and Wall Streeters and D.A.'s and streetwalkers, a late twentieth century urbanist's dream, says that when she heard Joe's voice it was like her mother waking her up in the morning.

Tears are in her eyes. She says, at the moment, she's feeling like she wants to hate her mother but she doesn't. Is this sentimentality or truth?

I think of the re-education camps for intellectuals, where they learn how to be as smart as the workers.

Is that, too, what we've got here?

Pol Pot. Mao.

Good for us. Good for them.

Though is there, was there, gentleness and attention to doubt in such camps? Like a bourgeois I rush to warn myself, "of course not, of course not." Though how do I know for sure?

"Stop." I hear the echoes of Joe's word. Go back. Sense.

My arm.

Back to work. While Bobby, sweet and sour, works in the galley. Is he scouring, is he oiling? I wonder about his mind. I wonder how it flies around. I feel guilty for having fucked Maisie. I feel crazy and in love with Bobby. My Talk story. Almost forgot. Philip. The three of us. Are we all queer?

Quick look at Laura's tits, do I get a hard-on? Yes.

Next case. Move on.

But I do have my friends, don't I?

Love is an action, let us not forget.

"Love" is bullshit. "Love" is pathology.

But "love" has always been pathology, in all the poems, Majnun and Laila and the troubadours. Denis de Rougemont, remember him, from college. Tristan and Iseult. All pathology, all "love," all something at least, worth hanging a life on, worth something.

Our circle of love.

Bullshit, bullshit, no. As much hate here as anywhere, and at least anger keeps it clean. Don't get mired in "love."

Or if you're going to get mired in "love," let it at least be for a "love" as pure as words can make it, a "love" of beauty itself, veiled and hinted at, that yes or no maybe or not held me in Philip Deschayne's apartment that first night I went.

Go back.

The wood. Another board.

A trip for sandpaper, across the room. Bend it to the block. Continue. Aching. No meal. The meal is late.

Midnight. Bobby still preparing the meal.

Baked potato. Caviar and sour cream.

We eat, we breathe, we are quiet, each little globe of salmon roe bursting as if in my brain like a bright orange balloon, then we talk.

The group talks. Various, but the sense of having only just begun. Familiar territory here. A man may do ten years in prison but be conscious for only seconds or minutes, adding up all the bits and pieces, the flashes and epiphanies. A way to look at it, anyway. So has each of us already done a five or ten year bit?

The plasticity of time, warped to our desires.

And space? What of it? Isn't there plenty of inner space to fly around in? If space is a really, really, really big box, or better yet those Russian nesting dolls, wouldn't there be space to fly around in one of those Russian nesting dolls?

Freedom from space. What a fine idea. Goes along with the other one, freedom from time, a boxed set.

What a lovely, thoughtful gift, thank you very much.

Go back. Come on. Come back. Give it all up. Sense.

My hand. Sand. Coffee. Fatigue.

By eight the sun has risen.

Carry on. The boards are my friend. I go inside one of their grooves, find a place for my mind to sleep. Cozy and warm, protected, the place for an animal, let winter go by, hibernate. Down here where my eyes see myself. Sawdust falling like snowflakes on my lair.

But when you wake up are you still in the *katzetlager?*

Eleven o'clock on the second day. Bad breath and Dunkin' Donuts. Take as many breaks as possible.

And now, what a bonanza. Joe calls a meeting to talk about how we're doing.

In the meeting I say all I'm glad about is this meeting. I say I'm at the point where being tired doesn't sand away my fantasies, it encourages them, my vigilance is gone. I feel like I'm showing off when I say this and I am.

Others also show off. Nearly everybody is showing off.

Except Bobby, who says nothing. Why is Bobby saying nothing? Joe asks. He asks it of Bobby, then of anyone else. Bobby looks glazed. His head is not down, he eyes Joe, he looks around the room, he smokes a cigarette, but he says nothing. Is he playing a game? Maybe he just doesn't want to show off, I say.

Or has he simply found a better way of showing off?

Bobby who knows how to make an entrance, who knows what a star turn is.

Joe asks Philip what he thinks. Philip with what sounds like a true believer's answer: "Probably he's angry."

"What do you feel?"

"He should wise up."

I hate that phrase, "wise up." Another of Joe's, dragged out from some '40s trunk, smelling of old celluloid and casual arrogance, I despair of Philip when he says such things, I cling to the hope that he says "wise up" only because he wants to hear what it sounds like in the air, wants to measure it and grade it and see how people react, even how Joe reacts and how he reacts to Joe; Philip as a holder of long questions, learning something or not.

Or is this my tattered fantasy, that my emotions continue to patch together, because he's my friend and if my friend doesn't fight and wonder like a Jew with God then what am I?

But what if Philip did fight, already, what if he did wonder once? He could have done it all in his deep, graceful mind and . . . satisfied himself?

Joe goes around the room. How to help Bobby. What to do with Bobby. Why don't we just leave him alone. Can't anyone just leave him alone?

Joe says we remind him of when he was a child, there was a kid who cried sometimes and the other kids could always make him cry, tears of rage, by telling him he was starting to cry even when he knew he was not, or wasn't anyway till they started on him.

I had a friend like that, too. I was almost that kid myself. I'm touched that Joe tells the story. It seems to be a story that condemns cruelty, or recognizes it anyway. Bobby stays quiet. As if he's unimpressed, as if he's gone deaf.

Joe shifts around who's doing what. I'm off the floor. I'm back to my beloved windows, which weren't really beloved until I spent a day sanding the floor. Windows that you can see through, windows that you can see an end of. Windows that put you out on the sill in the cold air. The dreams of the concentration camp, a slightly better job.

Who cares. Go back. Sense. The point of it all.

Will I make an "I" or won't I? Will "I" make an I or won't "I"?

When will all of this fall away? Nothing is falling away. I am secretly glad it's not falling away because if it all began to fall away I would be terrified and I myself would fall away. "I" myself would fall away.

The day is windy. Even at this height I am pelted by bits of trash and soot. I wear a jacket. I nurture hopes that the window cleaner will run out so that I'll have to go to the store for more. But it doesn't run out and anyway I find another, larger, refill bottle in the closet. I wash windows until it is dark and then I go back to sanding the floor.

Sense. Stop. Something is beginning to change. Once I come back inside, once my flat ass sits again on the floor, whole seconds go by without words in my head. The quiet is as sweet as water, and the very word "sweetwater" means something to me I never imagined it could mean.

Sweetwater Clifton, sweetwater who.

Sweetwater. Quiet. Running in my head. Change. Joe used to talk about change all the time, change is hard, he'd say, change is rare, change is slow until it is not. People don't want to change. You have to want to change. Words in my head again. Go back. Silence for a little longer. Sweetwater in my mouth, my saliva. The world is bright and sweet. My peripheral vision expands more easily. I can see the whole damn loft at once. I am so touched, in ways I cannot say. My chest burns dully, as though coals burned inside, embers in a brazier. Something is building. The sweet water of anticipation. Shapes take on depths they always had. How could I never have noticed? Furniture, walls, people. The air itself has more depth.

Joe comes by. Usually I'm someone he ignores. I am certainly not someone he dotes on. I feel his eyes in back of my shoulder, I sense his weight, his hairy arms, I've heard the creak of the boards, the halting of the creak of the boards, announcing his approach. I continue to sand. I see the fissures of the board, I see the cracks in the piece of sandpaper where it's been folded and folded again, I see my hand gripped like a claw and let it go. "Don't let me disturb you," Joe says.

"You're trying to steal my attention," I say, without moving my eyes, though they feel rigid and cease to really see.

"You're letting me," he says.

"Always a pleasure," I say.

"Cheers," Joe says, and moves away, in his wake the scent of roses.

I go back to work. I feel my resistance breaking down. But resistance to what? Is this brainwashing, after all? Dr. Droid, Dr. Void, Dr. J. the evil eye commies with their comic book . . . BRAINWASHING! Turning ordinary good Americans who one day if left in peace would water their lawns into filthy reds overnight.

The aroma of Bobby's cooking a second day. The sweetness of scallions in the wok, the sesame and ginger. *It won't be long now.* Or will it, the way time goes now? The scallions and ginger as if beckoning. Overwhelming. I've never desired ginger so much.

Hints of a finer food? Impressions, they say, are finer food.

Impression of Bobby with his wok, sober. I begin to wonder again, what he is about, how things work through him or not. I am astonished by my lack of perception. I can't even guess. Why not? Is he not my friend?

Don't do it, I tell myself, don't let him steal my attention, don't let myself even say it's he who would steal my attention, whether he would or not the buck stops here, it's I or "I" who must not let my attention be stolen. Go back. Look at Bobby. Smell his food, his seduction.

But sense. Sand. No words in head, to describe Bobby or myself or argue or have an opinion or critique or anything else. If I have something to say, I will say it, I will not rehearse it. Sand. Work. Lightly. Harder. This board, too, shall be clean.

My arm is getting stronger. I work the sandpaper back and forth. The sawdust flies up. I am getting stronger. "I" am getting stronger. I remember that I yearn for something. A hint of the beautiful, my mouth full of sweet water. My yearning makes me stronger. Or keeps me going anyway. Sand the wax and grime of decades away. Turn the sandpaper around, rearrange it on the block. See the pockets of resistance on the board. I have sanded here, now I'll sand there. I'll get it all, someday.

And then it's dinner on the second day.

CHAPTER 22

THE PLEASURES OF THE work.

The waft of garlic.

Vodka.

The smoky atmosphere around the television, the men watching the football.

Even thinking of us as "men."

The easy sexual confidence.

The tingling spine of defiance.

The *Bird Guide*.

The aura if not the reality of effortless superiority, continued.

Poverty's spare, clean embrace.

The sense of mind triumphing over body and so the banishing of disease.

And the banishing of dying?

Don't be obscene. Don't go crazy.

That's where all of this falls down.

Not the banishing of death, but the shy dance with death.

The play of fancy ideas.

Neither the banishing of irony nor the shy dance with irony, but the growth, in bitter, disputed ground, that we till and cultivate as best we can, of a few simple flowers. Crocuses, maybe. Lilies of the valley. Roses that you can't kill with a stick, thorny bushes that go on forever, you find them by the roadside, neglected for years, and coax them back to life.

*

The pleasure, too, of using the word "we." We did this. We felt that. As if "we" were not the greatest fiction of all.

*

A king calls a competition. "We" and "I" are summoned. The competition is to decide which is the greater fiction.

They joust, they battle, they grimace at each other, they do all the stuff, play the lyre, spout poetry.

A long, long time has passed, and the winner is not yet known.

*

Orphaned by the storm. So that Joe's apartment, and now this loft, become our orphanage.

*

Be bold. Leap. Damn the torpedoes! Full speed ahead!

Brave phrases, that you couldn't, or wouldn't, say in public, for fear of being mocked, or found out, or denigrated, or misunderstood, or put in proper perspective. The sanctity of a space where Joe could say such things. "Don't fire till you see the whites of their eyes." Another of Joe's favorites, brave, silly, sincere. It was his silly sincerity that in my exhaustion I liked best about him. It seemed so against good taste, so against reasoned compromise, putting a claim directly on your heart: as if once in a lifetime certain things must be said.

*

The pleasure, also, of the loft. It had the beauty, say, of the Brooklyn Bridge under construction, lithographs you see. The beauty of intention, imagining the whole of it from the part that hands and eyes have begun. The window frames being slowly painted their blues and greens. The relentless noise of the shop. Joe's particle board furniture, trimmed and clean, arranged around the big TV. The carpets with their image of prayer. Some day this place will be something, you say, it will be as bold as the man, and when it's finished he'll leave.

The pleasure of primary colors.

*

On the morning of the third day, I slept a little while. I sat down on a register and my chin fell into my neck. I was asleep ten or fifteen minutes, and I dreamt the whole time of waking up, of being awakened. Yet I awakened only into more layers of dream.

Finally I started snoring and Big Ronald shook my shoulder.

The third day was like an hallucination.

Joe forbade anyone to go out, for fear they'd be hit by cars.

I completed sanding one line of boards, the entire width of the loft. It wasn't great but it was "good enough." My mind began running out of things to say about itself. It either kept quiet or it ran on like a fizzling balloon, incomprehensible. I wasn't even sure in what proportions it was one thing or the other. I stopped winding my watch. My breath tasted like damp sawdust. The others seemed to move slower and slower, and I must have as well even if I wasn't viscerally aware of it. After awhile, I took a number of naps. Everyone did. Anytime anyone sat down, if they weren't smoking they were catching a few. Coffee more or less did its job. But we were trying to be two times awake, and our strength went fast.

"We," "our," fictions, but something like what it was. I have even fewer impressions of myself.

At meetings people mumbled.

Joe was staying awake, as well, because he said it was his responsibility, which when he said it and we were so tired made it seem as if he was blaming us, that it was our fault, our greedy need for supervision, that was causing him not to log his comfy eight or nine hours.

Bobby was quiet at every meeting, but in the galley he was a kind of maestro, furiously involved, turning out thirty plates of this, thirty plates of that. We ate off the dark blue plates every meal. Between meals Bobby washed them all, as if he really wanted to do it all, chief cook and bottle washer, master of beginning, middle, and end.

Meanwhile my frame of reference fell apart, a sea of peripheral vision flooded over it. It seemed to me that the whole loft and all its contents had become one big "we." The customary boundaries of "I" were there, but like broken lines, that on a map would indicate the most primitive sort of road, or a boundary between territories which no longer exist.

And then sometime on the morning of the fourth day, a sort of miracle. I began to feel stronger. This coincided with Joe asking me to help Bobby in the galley.

*

The pleasure of exhaustion.
The pleasure of wondering what comes next.
The pleasure of cigarettes.
The pleasure of doing.

*

The pleasure of standing beside Bobby, a little bit taller than he, a little bit jealous, listening to the creaks of the floorboards and the whispers of our blades as we slice through this or that.

CHAPTER 23

LAURA DEVELOPED SHOOTING PAINS in her leg so severe that she couldn't walk. Greg left with his fever at 106°. Nausea, nosebleeds, the severest sorts of migraines, symptoms you never heard of, anything that might get you out of there made an appearance. Mostly it was the simple exhaustion. Raoul gashed his hand in the service elevator doors. Others hallucinated and walked into walls. Almost as many took the week as a warning as took it for a challenge. By Sunday a third of us had left, and of those only a few returned. By comparison my "revival" made me feel jaunty. Maybe I wasn't so bad at this after all. Maybe I wasn't such a weakling worthless chicken coward . . . the words in my head were roughly formed, the words, really, of a boy. I was being boiled down. We all were. And all of us who made it from meeting to meeting expressed similar feelings of childish hope or pride. I started imagining myself a hero. Girls waving, parades. A phonograph record we found, in a stack of 78's, the day Joe took possession of the loft.

Lucky Lindy, hero of the USA. Were "we" all, when you got down to it, eight-year-olds?

For Sunday dinner Bobby has decided on white asparagus. He has found them in Chinatown somewhere and must have paid a mint. Joe peeled off cash to pay for them. Joe was never cheap, or if he'd been cheap once, because his father had the dry cleaners and it was the way things were, he'd overcome it. People could change; the living proof being the guy with the hairy blond forearms in his Sears short-sleeve shirt.

But why had Joe changed?

Because he had more self-hatred than any of us, I propose to myself. The ritualized words of half-remembrance run roughshod over me. "Stop." "Go back." "Gently." I hear Joe's voice from the first Saturday afternoon in his apartment, baritone, inviting, unashamed. His words are in me and I can't stop them. I can't stop anything. And yet everything, if not stopping, is at least slowing down.

My thoughts of Joe are like a drunk's slurs. Are they thoughts or are they wishes?

I wash the asparagus. The tap water chills my fingers. I dry them with paper towels as though each piece of the paper towel is precious. In silence Bobby shows me how to snap the tough stalk off the tender part. He's like a mime, his gestures exaggerated and simple, as if he were talking to a foreigner, and he has the slender frame of a mime. The day has turned out blue and crisp. The sun glances through the loft's east windows teasing our exhaustion.

Come out and play. Come read the Sunday paper. A museum maybe? A walk in the park?

It is the duty of my mind to know where the stalks should be snapped. My mind, not my fingers, feels the bend in the stalk, the snapping point, the resistance, the point where living ends and dead begins. I mustn't waste an inch of stalk. I mustn't waste a quarter of an inch; less; infinitesimal, what my mind's eye alone can see. This is what I am looking for: my mind's eye, my mind's hand.

I put the saved stalks in a pan and the dead bits in a pile. For a moment I believe in myself, but Bobby turns from his sauce and looks my way laughing and then I believe nothing. "Is this all right?" I look—with a quivering forehead—but I do not say. "Good enough," Bobby looks—with bovine eyes, at the pan—but he does not say. He doesn't show me all over again how to do it, so it must be so.

The sorcerer's apprentice. Ah, there's a sweet phrase.

What about the sorcerer's apprentice's apprentice?

My mind is like a board sanded almost clean or anyway I would like to think so. I mock myself for thinking about boards at all. I mock myself for mocking myself. Maisie. How did it happen that now my eyes are following Maisie? She passes by. What's she doing? She's wearing a sweatshirt that says "Yale Crew." Where did that come in, what blast from the past? The sweatshirt gives a plumpy reassurance to her shape. Stage 1, Stage 2, Stage 3. Does Hodgkin's really go away? If I think about Hodgkin's am I trying to kill her? If I think "am I trying to kill her" am I trying to kill myself? We walk in mirrors, you and I, Maisie. But why do I say "you and I"? What's so special about "you and I"? Living a past that isn't passed. Fool's paradise, awash in sentimentality. Be real. Maisie in my peripheral vision going to the closet by the elevator, slowed, self-conscious, swimming in the air of the place. Maisie solid and un-bowed, the back of her, her hair, the parts of Maisie that don't bother saying good-bye.

I am done with my asparagus. I am going to put them away. Stacking one paper towel on the other I become aware, as if from a suddenness in a still sky, a shooting star or was it, of the milky flash of her face. I allow myself to look her way, on the half-argued ground that if I'm consciously looking how can my attention be stolen? She's by the closet, paused, as if Joe had shouted "Stop!," looking directly at me with a blankness that could be fatuity or love or the sheer exhausted mistakenness of eyes that have to land somewhere. I look back at her as though it was more than luck. Our eyes hold. What's this? Her eyes like still green pools, her curiosity, our surprise, but before I begin to know what it is she looks away. A spell snapped or it was nothing to start with or she feels embarrassed for her lapse. I return perfunctorily to my paper towels, my asparagus, my job, my "self," but I feel like a sixth grader now, moony, all the eroticism in my world reduced to looking, to stares, to one set of eyes; as if it were she one more time or is this the last brightening ember? She brings a stepladder from the closet. She's indifferent to me again. Where's she going with the ladder, what's she doing with it now, carrying it in her arms as if it were an overgrown child? She doesn't look at me, I'm nowhere in her thoughts. The shame of my mistake suffuses me, but I'm also skewered by longing, as though these two strong emotions, having plotted my ambush, attack from opposite directions.

Go back. Gently. Give it a shot at least, let your longing take you where it will, feed the childish hunger in your eyes.

With what? Feed it with what, I ask, you ask, Joe's disembodied baritone asks, my father asks, my mother asks, like a mother whose cupboard is bare.

Learn to live with it then, let it drool and wonder. And Bobby? Consider Bobby, whisking his hollandaise or whatever he will call it right next to you. Has Maisie looked at him? I don't think so. Is Bobby aware? Of course he's aware. He whisks his sauce as if it were the stuff that dreams are made of. She walks past the galley and her breeze causes the muscles of his neck to ripple. We are all so tired. A little later there are tears in his eyes.

Maisie has brought out the stepladder so that she can paint the ceiling. Who told her to do this I cannot guess. Nobody else is painting the ceiling, yet it's in our plans, in our playbook. I imagine Maisie wants a moment when she can feel like she is reaching for the heavens, the happy feeling of the world looking upside down. I indulge myself with such fantasy, but do not look her way, not directly anyway. I arrange my chores so that she's enough in my line of sight that I remain aware of her, like Icarus falling from the sky in the Bruegel, unnoticed and noticed at once, the artist seeing what the world does not. A quart of paint sits on the top step of her ladder like a crown she's put aside. Her feet are on the third step and she's already, in her hair and on her sweatshirt, flecked with what looks like snow. Her brush is painting the sky, making it pure again. More paint droplets fall. She's put newspapers on the floor around her. Her hand with its brush waves slowly, her eyes wave slowly, she's aware of each mistake. Maisie stretched out thin so that her sweatshirt comes up and her torso is revealed, beige and taut, a prize in a box of candy. Bobby leaves the galley as if in a dream and walks over to her. She seems to pay him no mind. She dips her brush in the can and paints the tin heaven. Bobby stands beside the ladder looking up like a man who's seen something in a tree. Time passes. Maisie continues to ignore him. Her reach takes her on one journey then another, journeys to unpainted portions of tin. Is she becoming unbalanced? Bobby takes hold of the ladder to steady it, then lets go as if realizing his lie and his presumption. A gobbet of paint falls off her brush, splashing his hair and forehead and dribbles down.

I am aware that my own feelings for Maisie are gone forever. My co-conspirator who never was. But Bobby, what of him?

At two we eat in silence, the clatter of forks on plates competing only with the taxis and wind-rattled windows and whatever internal monologues our enfeebled minds are still capable of engendering. As usual after the meal we have a meeting to discuss whatever's come up. There isn't much now, people seem afraid to waste energy on speaking, a hoarding instinct is taking hold. Valerie mentions this. No one comments. No one seems interested in smartass remarks, or criticism. Big Ronald says he's had a nervous stomach for days but now has become thoroughly nauseated and suspects it's something he ate. A congenial topic at last, complaints about food and upset stomachs fly. The culprit is suspected to be the morning donuts from Ramon's, didn't the banana creams in particular have a sulfury smell about them and in addition they tasted off, a little bit sweet-and-sour. Big Ronald feels sicker just from people talking about it. For most of this discussion I'm feeling simply glad it's nothing I chopped up. When people are through speculating Joe weighs in. He speaks with the calibrated informality of someone accustomed to having the last word. He says what's going on with Ronald goes on of course all the time, people are always getting upset stomachs from the last meal they can remember or that's what they think, anyway, but actually it's all bullshit, it's all in their minds, chalk another one up for fantasyland, because he was just reading an article in *Scientific American* and the food you eat doesn't really get to your GI tract where all the trouble starts for twenty-four or thirty-six hours, so actually it really is all bullshit, how can you get an upset stomach from things that aren't even in your stomach yet? Joe loves finding out that things are bullshit. Big Ronald stirs his neck, his diagnostic grin settles out, he lights a Newport to get control of his breath. Others trim their sails accordingly. Val contributes her view that that was a really interesting article that Joe was talking about, it confirms other research she's read. A kind of bidding war is begun and now others as well remember that they've heard something confirming Joe's insight. Julie asks if it's a case of cognitive dissonance. Others think it isn't. This spurs Joe to start in about other studies he's read, about digestive medicines, which show that Tums are about as good as anything. "It's all bullshit, it's all in your mind—" He hesitates, "until it isn't." I hate the hesitation. I think of the Wizard of Oz. Yet I concede to myself that Joe doesn't really ram immensity down your throat. He actually has the minor gift of talking about trivialities without making them seem bigger than they are. He simply likes small things; gypsy music and minor keys. We then fall appreciatively, and exhaustedly, silent. For some reason I notice Bobby sitting with his hands in his lap and his legs nicely apart, as though he could sit this way discreetly protecting his private parts for a hundred years and no Buddha would complain. And as I watch him it's kind of crazy—is he doing it for my benefit?—Bobby's face crimsons and his eyes billow wide and round as if he's a balloon being blown up. "Asparagus pee," he says.

"What about it?" Joe senses the challenge in the choked fewness of Bobby's words, which come out barely bitten off.

Bobby harvests a breath. "What you're saying, I don't care who wrote it, it's wrong, or maybe you misunderstood it—two hours after you eat asparagus your piss smells like it."

The room titters uneasily, in nervous recognition. But Joe isn't amused. His eyes narrow in their Charlie Chan way. He taps a cigarette out of its packet. "It's different," he says, with such certainty one can almost feel it as wind.

"What's different? It's not different." Tears rim Bobby's eyes now. He's like a kid protesting a bad call in a game.

"One's a liquid," Joe reasons.

"It all goes in your stomach."

Joe shifts tactics, lightens up. "Is there a doctor in the house?" he calls.

"It's bullshit," Bobby says.

"Calm down. Take it easy."

"Asparagus piss!" Bobby shouts, like a kid again, one who's just discovered his big voice and is ready to shout down the world. "Asparagus piss!"

The others, including myself, know what this is about. We think we do, anyway, we think it's about right and wrong and hit and miss and denial and truth and while you're at it throw in faith and disbelief and trust and mistrust as well. And having a sense of humor about life, and is something happening to that too, is it dying in the dregs of these days? But no one says any of that. No one jumps in. No one takes sides.

It's possible that a kind of sadistic glee was taking hold of us then. Asparagus piss! It's true!

Philip, like one of the wise men holding up the world, takes it on himself to say something that to me sounds facetious but maybe is simply an exhausted mind trying to be helpful: "What Bobby's saying would only apply if you were asparagus positive, which of course not everybody is."

I feel as sorry for Philip now as when Diane's boyfriend was pounding on me and he stood there as helpless as a calf with the take-out coffee in his hand. My eyes canvas the room. Faces as blank as the proverbial *tabula rasa*. Are people sensing? Have they given up? Joe sits smoking his Newport with an air of purposeful distraction, as if remembering a movie where the natives had the white hunter in a pot, and the white hunter knew he mustn't show fear.

We return to work. I wash the dishes with Bobby. When the bubbles of the detergent start baptizing my hands, I know I've begun to go insane. The tears rimming Bobby's eyes remain, their gloss pink and inconsolable. When the dishes are done I go back to the floor. I sand with a rhythm that is mechanical and hypnotic, the way I'd learned to screw certain girls who were afraid of male feeling. Back and forth, back and forth, I suppose I could be jerking off as well, and get just as little pleasure. I am putting in time. Time meanwhile is doing its utmost not to cooperate. Joe shuffles around as though nothing has happened. He is wearing his slippers again. Five stepladders now dot the loft, oil rigs or Towers of Babel, take your pick. I lose track of Bobby again. I may even be watching the sway of Laura's swank ass on her ladder—for what more spiritual contemplation than that could one find on the afternoon of the fifth day?—when Bobby's voice, a little far off, breaks through the concerto of sandpaper and saws, like a patron making a fuss in a theater several rows away. As his voice comes closer, I turn. Why not? Steal my attention! Go ahead, take my wife, please! He is dogging Joe's steps, while Joe pretends with what seems like good-natured patronization that Bobby isn't even there. "Asparagus piss! Get it? Admit it! Why can't you admit one thing?"

People are stopping now, all over the loft, though I observe that Philip does not, he continues washing his window with grave sincerity. He looks like an athlete playing with pain. While Maisie seems bored with it all.

Joe puts on his trench coat and presses for the elevator. Bobby turns towards the rest of us. "Losers! Mediocrities! You all ought to be seeing shrinks! He doesn't have anything! What does he know? Asparagus pee!"

For a moment I can't figure out what he's doing but what it is is he's unzipping his fly and presently he starts pissing on a slab of the unredeemed floor. The pungent woody perfume of whatever's the acid in asparagus reaches at least as far as me. Bobby's pee puddles on the darkening boards. When the doors of the elevator open, Joe must have second thoughts about whatever his previous plan was and hauls Bobby, with a sweeping arm gesture that's like a vaudeville hook, inside the elevator with him. The doors shut. Shortly—how long? Thirty seconds? A minute?—they reopen as though someone's played a joke, as though the elevator has gone nowhere. Bobby emerges first, with his fly zipped. None of us know what if anything was said in the elevator, said or done or imagined. Joe takes his trench coat off, hangs it on a hook like a '40s detective back in the office. His features are bland now, and relaxed, as they get sometimes when he watches movies all night and his belly is finally full of them.

Bobby goes right to sanding the floor, on boards next to mine, his eyes still moist. Both of us begin to sand like demons. Or is "demon" the proper word? Does "demon" connote too much? "Go back." "Gently." To whatever you've got left of yourself, to your fear, your terror, sand your terror away. But how could either of us have arms so strong? I feel like I am coming irrevocably close to where I'd never wanted to be. How would I get back, Bobby? Bobby? Would you see me through? Everything feels too late, but I sand like a demon and so does he. The evening passes. We take no breaks. Our sections of board link together, then link up with others, continents of freshly sanded wood are coming into being. The world smells fresh. Our land is unadorned. The room shimmers. The others in it I begin to see as if I were wearing 3-D glasses. When they reach an arm in my direction I expect they're about to punch me. If their faces come my way I expect a kiss. Or do I really? "Really" is in short supply. Another night goes by. Cal puts a post-it on his shirt that reads "wake me if I pass out." I further my infatuation with sandpaper. It's the one-fifty I love now, its surface as smooth as skin. Yet what miracles it performs! It sands away sin! In its caress, the trampled upon, the ruined, the slicked and painted, are reborn. I feel the smallness of myself, reduced to the space between the windows and the galley. What relevance has bigness now? In smallness, in the country of the sanded boards, I shall find freedom or become very scared by its prospect. What if this is all I need?

I fall down on the floor at four o'clock. I do not even know I'm falling asleep. It seems like I'm simply talking to myself, telling myself to stop, telling myself to go back, telling myself to sense. When I wake up Bobby's head is on my shoulder. He's fallen asleep as well. Day has broken. There's rain in the eastern sky, rain or snow, the grayness of beginnings. Maisie is looking down at both of us. She's on her knees. "Open your eyes, sleepypeep," she says to Bobby. He lifts himself from my shoulder. He looks like he might say, like a boy in a myth, "Where am I?" For a second I imagine I know something about an angel.

Maisie gets up and goes back to work. Bobby and I sit there for awhile.

CHAPTER 24

SO WE RAN AFTER the impossible and nothing happened. That's what it seemed like, anyway. But what does it mean when "nothing" happens, isn't that what we were looking for, "nothing" to happen? Isn't "nothing" the impossible?

I managed to say something like that to Joe at one of the meetings on the fifth day. He snorted and refolded his legs. "Suffer," was all he said.

Was Joe getting off easy? Those cryptic little remarks, that parodists could do shtick all day with. But Ty Duncan was a parodist, and he didn't laugh out loud or groan. It was one thing to make fun and another thing to be serious, and the premise of our life here was to know which went when. So Joe got a pass on "Suffer." Our minds bent around the word, searched for its cracks, emulated its strength. Such was the idea, anyway, though whether any of us had enough left to do it was an open question. And anyway, long, rolling, strenuous sentences on topics ineffable and unnamable were targets just as large if not larger. Say too much when nothing can be said. Or, say nothing at all and die.

At another of the meetings, Maisie said she finally realized what had made her sick. Sort of a showstopper; then she said, "Cancer."

"Funny, that's what I found out too," Joe said.

His voice like a deep well, with a surprise of feeling at the bottom. As if he was not only protecting her but leaving it obvious for once, the way an underappreciated uncle might. Had I misconstrued Joe? Only once had I seen Joe touch Maisie, the time they danced. Did he love her, in his fashion? Love her the way he loved everybody?

Sometimes those that are near . . .

Maisie came here so that Joe could help her: had I forgotten?

I'd forgotten nothing. Not just now, not on this subject anyway. But I wondered.

The tangling up of the personal with everything else.

Was Joe *sweet* on her?

He announced an interruption of the work, a New Year's Eve party. But it was hardly a real announcement because we were all already aware of it. Some of the Boston group were coming down. And there were going to be visitors from Berkeley, people we wouldn't know, but Joe was thinking of setting up a second group out there. This last was the real announcement. Maybe Philip knew something about this, maybe Maisie or Bobby or Liddie, but to most of us it was an utter surprise, like an only child considerably grown up hearing that his parents were having a baby. Joe went on to remind us that the event itself was continuing, just as war was the continuation of diplomacy by other means so we should consider the party a part of the event, a chance to observe our exhausted selves and others in a different context for a few hours. Use all the pig including the squeal.

He sent Bobby and I out for the booze. I hadn't been outside for a week, but it could as easily have been a month of Sundays for how unnerved I was by the rush of humanity. I felt like I'd be run over. I felt barely able to resist. How small I was, how small we were, Bobby and I, even with our secrets. The wind gusted. I swept my scarf across my face. Eighth Street with its usual mix of shoppers and hustlers, some of the latter of whom I was certain I'd seen before, lingering in the underlit corridors of the courts or standing beside second-rate lawyers to cop a plea, brought me up short: I suddenly felt like a released prisoner, like these guys I'd been putting in jail. I felt not so much a gush of empathy as what seemed a more useful reversal of fortunes. Why was I working at the D.A.'s office, aside from Joe's prodding, aside from all the explanations I supplied, the low pay, the Ivy League ease-of-access? So that I could have before me an image of what a prisoner was! I said this to Bobby in a rush. I told him to look around.

"Why'd you take a job, then, where you're locking people up?" Bobby asked.

It was a question I thought I'd already answered, but when he said it I wanted to cry.

It seemed like everyone in New York who'd got off work early was in Astor Liquor stocking up. The checkout lines stretched back into the liqueurs where Bobby and I sat as if stalled in rush hour traffic with our shopping cart full of everything Philip would need for another punch. Joe had peeled off two hundred dollar bills and I was feeling giddy again, with my fatigue, my freedom, the money in my pocket. But Bobby, since deflecting—that's really what it was, a deflection—my outburst on the street, had turned quiet. Normally it was he who was given to flourishes and I who taciturnly absorbed them. What had brought about the reversal?

A little later I thought I knew. While we waited in line a guy I knew from the courthouse came in. He was a court officer in one of the arraignment parts downstairs, kind of a large guy, big enough to be a cop, with a mustache that looked too small for him, that made his face look slightly squeezed. Dan something, good-natured enough, but I had no intention of more than nodding his way. I kept things proper downtown. I didn't go out and drink with anybody, except for Diane when there was Diane. And I had an aversion to mixing anything about my "inner" life with my job. Too much to explain. Impossible to explain. I wore my job like a cloak, to keep out the rain. Dan saw me, gave a little mock-salute which I answered with my nod, then seemed to settle himself, with a hand basket, in the aisle in back of the liqueurs. It was then Bobby said, "I'm learning how to fly."

I assumed he meant fly a plane, wondered for a moment where he was getting the money, but—conscious of not expressing negative emotions—I put enthusiasm rather than skepticism into my voice: "Great! Really? Where?"

"Nowhere," he said. "Inside myself."

"Oh. I thought you meant a plane."

"No. No plane. Me." He said it as though he'd been thinking about telling someone for awhile. His eyes went into the shopping cart. He picked up the Cointreau and peered at the label.

I felt uneasy on account of his seriousness. I attributed it, I supposed, to our lack of sleep. Perhaps I wasn't even hearing him right. But I hesitated before asking him to elaborate because I didn't want Dan in the next aisle to start picking up bits of this crazy conversation and hear my voice mixed up in it. I said nothing more. Bobby started peeling the label off the Cointreau before we'd even bought it. Nothing more was said about flying. I was so tired I half-forgot about it.

But at one point later, when I was sanding again and half-remembered, what passed through my mind like a verbal phantom was the title of Ouspensky's book about Gurdjieff, *In Search of the Miraculous.*

Had Bobby stumbled on a bit of the miraculous?

The party started around nine. Everyone went home and changed their clothes. The loft was half-painted and a quarter of its floor was sanded. Wherever we were at seven o'clock: "Stop!" "Good enough." It had started to snow shortly after dark and the snow made curtains on the windows and on Broadway the traffic went away. People trudged around. It would be a trudging-around New Year's Eve, snow in people's shoes and smiles on their faces. In the galley of the loft sat a pot of mulled wine, and a bowl with Philip's punch. Everything felt crystalline and fresh, life brought to a glow by blowing gently on it, holding out against the snowy dark encroachment.

The carload from Boston arrived. A little like country cousins, but there was a good-looking guy with a razory smile, thin-lipped, short hair, who I was sure had slept with Maisie. He looked at her as though he'd never quite given up possession and she looked at him as though to say "what an asshole." The country cousins liked to dance. The green carpets were up. The thin-lipped guy danced with Maisie a couple of times and she didn't look at him much but their rhythms were the same and I wondered how much there might have been between them. Once Joe cut in, the Boston guy dropped away. At around ten the Berkeley contingent showed. And because a number of people from our group who'd dropped out of the "event" returned for the party, the loft began to fill up. Joe had commissioned

Greg to make a dance tape for the occasion, and the result was punk not the Washboard Rhythm Kings, or punk and the Washboard Rhythm Kings. Conference of the Eclectics.

Philip had "cooked up another doozy." His phrase, again. Only Bobby and I, besides Philip, knew exactly what was in it, but many passed it by on spec as if it were Jim Jones' Kool-Aid. People were tired enough, giddy enough, without it. The room smelled of fresh clothes for the first time in a week. Our guests from Berkeley were mostly in their twenties, more athletic-looking than ourselves. I chatted up a pretty girl who turned out to be a dancer in an Oakland troupe, and she told me what some of the others did, they were carpenters and construction guys and mechanics and one guy with an idea for an outer space epoxy that he was cooking up in his garage. Not one was a Berkeley student. But I did recognize an older woman, maybe forty, lined face and a ponytail, eyes a little too bright. She had visited Joe once before, over the summer, a sort of mystery woman though Val, who knew so many people, knew her from somewhere; and now she was accompanied by a tall dark balding guy who from appearances in his younger days might have been a Pakistani cricket star but who wasn't Pakistani at all, his name was Rothenberg, he'd grown up in Minneapolis, and he was the left brain/right brain psychologist about whom Philip had written, the guy with the connection to the Sufis in London and Marrakech. This couple that wasn't really a couple hung back with Joe and Maisie and Philip as if they were the adults chaperoning the party. They drank Philip's punch and sat around, and it looked like the psychologist was telling stories, or gossiping. Some of the others from Berkeley paid deference to the woman as we paid deference to Joe, and from this accumulation of gestures it finally dawned on me what must be going on here: the woman, or the left brain/right brain guy, had invited Joe to come out and take over her group. It was as if at some point, maybe over the summer, the woman had acknowledged Joe's suzerainty, or anyway that she could learn something from him. Three cheers for the home team, we're number one, big index fingers stirring the air. But what would it mean if Joe started going out to Berkeley? What would happen to us? For a moment my mind raced through its Freudian archives in a kind of rushed defense of the realm, and what emerged was an unstable powder of separation anxiety and oedipal longings to murder.

People danced lethargically until they didn't, then everything was more or less frenzy. It was only we, the New York hosts, who hadn't rested all week. Not a few of us slept through all of it in the corners, curled up like dogs. Why not? We'd be back at work tomorrow. I couldn't imagine who would be adhering to Joe's dictum to keep sensing as if the event was continuing, maybe Bobby was; I sensed myself, but only because I'd got so used to doing it that I couldn't have stopped if I'd tried. That's how things were then.

I had never liked to dance, but I would dance if I thought it would get me laid. This seemed the case with the California girl, the girl in the Oakland troupe. In part I danced with her just to show Maisie I didn't care. How grown-up, how evolved. The girl, Austin, danced circles around me but she seemed to like my dour little gravitas, maybe she thought it was a New York thing. Or maybe it was the amount she drank. Neither of us was afraid of the punch. Bobby joined in and eventually, after midnight and nobody turned into a pumpkin or a saint, we went outside. Six or seven inches had fallen. We sat in the snow in the middle of Broadway. Strangers tromped around like pioneers. One group had plastic cups and a bottle of cheap champagne and they passed out drinks, to whomever, as they partied up the block. The traffic lights still worked, though they had nothing to direct, like the famous trees that fall in forests where no one hears. The snow still came down, light and steady, an airy benediction. Austin had never seen anything like it. Neither Bobby nor I had the heart to tell her we hadn't either. She shivered and loved it and I leaned over as we sat in the street as if I was about to kiss her but pushed snow down her neck instead. Children, children. Why not? It had been an awfully long week.

Bobby told us a story. He was sitting in the street as well. The story was too complicated for me to make sense of but it had knights in it and the Hundred Years' War and at a certain point I realized it was the story he'd drawn on the lamppost on Mount Auburn Street in Cambridge. In the story there was a jester, and whatever heads or tails I could make of all the other characters, their trappings, their comings and goings on the historical stage, I knew that in the very private Dungeons & Dragons of my friend's fevered mind the jester was the only good one. Bobby wasn't half-finished telling it when a bus came along, tires slashing for traction, wipers flailing, looming out of the north with one headlight on and one gone off, a lost cyclops plodding its way to nowhere.

We hugged ourselves and hoped it would miss us and it did, but we didn't move.

In fact we didn't move till Joe came down. He had his trench coat on and Dr. Rothenberg with a striped scarf wound around him like an Oxford don and Maisie and Philip and the woman with the ponytail and too bright eyes. The grown-ups were going to look for something to eat. It was maybe two A.M. Rothenberg said something to Austin that had familiarity in it, and she got up and said she would like to get something to eat as well. Bobby and I also got up. Austin was too wise in the ways of things to ask us if we wanted to come. This she would leave to the nabobs, none of whom said anything to us, maybe Joe was still pissed at Bobby from the day before, but anyway we stayed. They went off into the whiteness of the night. After half a block we couldn't see them.

Bobby said to me, "This sucks. He's eating us. I'm eaten. We're already dead."

"Not quite," I said.

"We're food for him," Bobby said. "My head's bitten off. I've got to escape."

"You won't get far if your head's bitten off," I said.

"We're already dead," he said.

CHAPTER 25

BOBBY AND I WALKED up to Washington Square, where the drug dealers were having snowball fights, then we drifted, silently, back to the loft and back to the floor. In the hours between four and seven others trickled in as well, including Joe, who arrived with three plump ducks in a shopping bag that he was making a fuss about. Chinatown, somebody had ducks. Now Bobby could make Peking duck. Bobby looked sober and put the ducks in the refrigerator. Maisie was beside Joe with a bit of snow on her nose and in her hair. The heat of the elevator hadn't quite melted it off. They looked like a king and a queen. Indeed the thought arose in me, floated in half-formed words that I noted while chasing them off: is this what this group was all about, to satisfy our human longing for monarchs? What a joke that one would be. Maisie took off her coat and went behind the partition where Joe's bed lay. I followed Bobby's eyes that followed her then froze at the point of her inevitable disappearance.

Others cleaned up. I sanded. Which is to say I moved my arm back-and-forth, applied such-and-such pressure, listened to the hissing and shushing of the abrasive on the encrusted board, saw the dust grow on my fingers, contemplated this anti-habit as habit. What did you expect, if not the eternal return? I had lost weight and my stomach was in upheaval and my vision was mildly doubled and I loved every one of my symptoms. Proof I'd done something, anyway. Proof I hadn't just sat here and moved my arm.

But in the exhaustion of not only my body but my ambition, something peculiar developed on this last day. Emotions, strong emotions, I'd seldom felt, or not felt for a long time, arose in me. Joy then sadness then joy then sadness, in me who usually was neither a joyful nor a sad man, who was angry and fearful if anything; nor was there really any cause of these emotions excepting the "causes" that sat there everyday. Having said good-bye to my parents in more or less definitive terms, I now remembered them teaching me how to bike-ride, a summer day, their togetherness then, the buzzing of the bees, my cream-and-red Schwinn, my mother's hopefulness then. Joe's cancer, losing a ball, no words, Maisie's cancer. Sickness old age death the whole shot. Where had they been hiding? Let sadness go. Let gladness go. Sense. Look. Listen. And my sadness came back double, for Bobby who didn't get Maisie and watched her go with frozen eyes and Louie who didn't get her either and didn't even know what he'd missed; then my joy redoubled, too, just for my ability to feel redoubled sadness. A virtuous circle but why say "virtuous," why not "circle," why anything at all, why words? These three fat ducks, somehow, in Joe's imagining like the breaking of the atonement fast and so was he not a kike from Brooklyn after all, you can take the kike out of Bensonhurst, put him on a train Manhattan-bound, write a '20s song or a '30s song, but "kike from Brooklyn" will he remain. Joy and sadness.

All of it as if it had been hidden under canvas in the dark. In a box put away, like my grandmother's preserves.

Go back. Sense. Yeah, yeah, yeah. Like the Beatles' "yeah," or just yeah?

Bobby stayed sullen through the day. I blamed him for it, as if his sourpuss, or soberpuss, somehow threatened the excited cycling of my joy and sadness.

At four o'clock Joe called a last meeting, to see where we were winding up or if something might still be done. Greg had found a lamp in a niche, and this seemed to make Joe happy. Phyl said one thing she learned, she was never going to whore again, one more bullshit irrelevant saccharine lie which inexplicably made me want to cry. False hopes, odd dreams. A home for silliness. There should be such places. Refuges from the world's blind purpose. Or so it seemed, anyway, sitting there on the bench. The cruelties inflicted on people with flat asses. We knew nothing, but who did. Calm down. The end is near.

I thought I might say, might report upon, my adventures in joy and sadness, but then thought better of it—"showing off," "too rehearsed"—and then spoke anyway about trying not to speak. Joe looked at me as if I made life hard for myself. "What is it you really want to say?" he asked. I felt choked up. The room spun around. Joe's head seemed enormous, like the head of a jack-in-the-box, coming out of the sky. Nothing at all came to me to say. I who was so full of words. "Don't worry about it," he said. "Maybe next time."

Val spoke. Ty spoke. Liddie spoke. The preciousness of their voices. What of it? A week of this. Ugly breath in the room. Yet, the preciousness of their voices. I struggled to hear. Finally Bobby, who was dour still, said he'd spoiled the plum sauce. Joe reached into his corduroy pants in his silent movie way, as though the card would read "Money solves everything!" and snapped off a twenty from the fold of bills in his pocket and told me to go to Chinatown and buy plum sauce. He gave me an address of a place he was sure would be open, and I left.

*

What happened in the hour or hour and a quarter that followed I pieced together from others. The meeting continued and there were words, that Philip described as a bit of urinary Olympics, between Bobby and Joe. Joe teased Bobby about spoiling the plum sauce, and Bobby went along with it awhile, teasing himself until it wasn't himself any longer that he was teasing but Joe for putting him in the galley in the first place. Was it another little gap in Joe's understanding that he'd thought Bobby could make plum sauce without screwing it up? Wasn't it Joe's responsibility to protect us from danger? Bobby said it all with smiles, Philip said. They would have been his first smiles of the day.

But Joe was not amused, and I suppose I thought, afterwards, why should he have been?

But shouldn't he have known what to say, or do?

Maybe he did.

Maybe he didn't.

Maybe there are some things no one knows.

Joe said to Bobby, "Sit still and eat your spinach."

"I already ate it," Bobby said.

"I don't know what to tell you then," Joe said, and that was the end of it.

People just wanted it to be over then. The week, the "event," all of it. They didn't care who won.

A little like the wisdom that soldiers get if they're on the losing side.

There are beauties in defeat.

There will be other days.

Giving up. Hands up. Submission. Freedom.

Did a cone of power arise then?

Did we become more than ourselves?

But how could I know?

And I wasn't there.

And anyway who talks about such things? Naifs and the broken-hearted.

Joe said, "We'll eat at seven," and in truth they did, they started without me because the store Joe sent me to was closed and I had to hustle around Mott and Bowery for another and in the meantime Bobby found a bit of old plum sauce in the refrigerator door, so there was that.

Everyone seemed so relaxed, Philip said later. Jokes about the floor, which now looked like somebody's skin rash. Ty would rent a sander tomorrow, even things out in no time. He smoked a pipe for the first time all week. A plate with the crisp skin of the duck, a bowl with the scallions, another plate with the pancakes, a cup of sauce. Bobby offered all of these as if proudly, and a little like a benediction. But no one praised the food because no one ever did, you were supposed to eat and breathe and sense and there was still time and the chance.

For what, Bobby?

He ate a pancake or two. Not bad if I say so myself.

That was his look, anyway. Mischievous, Philip said.

Enjoying a fine feedbag.

But where was Louie with the rest of the plum sauce? Joe was getting annoyed.

He praised the food.

Compliments to the chef.

Bobby said it, not Joe.

Or did he say it with a question mark?

Too much. Go back. Gently. Sense.

We would sleep well tonight.

The nightmare of life? Oh, please!

We are a garden that feeds our selves. We have gardens within us.

Joe got up to put the TV on. It was still New Year's, after all. Bowl games. The Orange Bowl was on, Oklahoma and Nebraska that year. The women looked bored, the men like silly stereotypes revived or pretending to be. No one really noticed—someone on the screen was completing a thirty yard pass—when Bobby made a run at the windows, or rather Big Ronald noticed because he was coming back from the toilet, but by then Bobby had flung the window up with such abandon that the old glass shattered and he was clambering onto the ledge as the shards rained down on him. Big Ronald shouted Bobby's name and ran his way. Bobby crouched like an actor playing a bug-boy in a film. Others stood and turned and started. Joe yelled "Stop!" Big Ronald lunged for one of his legs to grab hold of as Bobby sprang. Nobody saw his last expression.

I was returning up Bleecker Street with the plum sauce in my hand. A cab had let me off at Lafayette because Bleecker was badly plowed. I felt a whoosh that was like a dancer in the dark. I hadn't time to think. He landed on the sidewalk just ahead of me.

*

The way he landed, the way he looked, I won't describe. Mostly because I won't get it right. I'll use too many words. But it was a mess.

And a hint of the obscene: there was something beautiful, as well. There always is.

*

The police came, not all that fast. The holiday, the storm. They took statements. I gave mine. I told the truth. Everybody did. What else was there to tell? Though everyone had trouble describing what the group was, what was going on upstairs. "Therapy," was what most said. A few said, "watching football," but then had to elaborate so the cops wouldn't think there was a contradiction. Each explanation seemed to me as close as the other; just coming from different angles.

Upstairs the shattered window was still thrown open. It was a window that I had washed. My window, my love. As clean, as clear, as starlight. The wind wound through the loft. The rest of the Peking duck sat on plates. No one touched the window frame or swept the broken glass until the cops said we could. Joe said little. He looked surprised. The only one weeping was Philip.

*

Letter from Bobby.

To Whom It May Concern & You Know Who You Are:

I wished there was a letter from Bobby.
I wished there was something.

Sincerely yours.

*

But he did send me a dream. Maybe an arch way of putting it,
but it's how it still seems.

In the dream I am Bobby. I-who-am-Bobby am getting ready
to fly. I know how to fly. Or I think I know how to fly. I'm fairly
sure. A chance.

I am in the loft. So are the others. They're having their meeting. Their backs to me, their cigarette smoke rising. Will they care,
will they be amazed?

Neither rage nor defeat touch my soul. How can they, I am a
fly-boy, tousle-haired and free.

But also, if I turn around and think about it, like Woody Allen
with that big thing on from *Bananas*? That too, maybe. Vaudeville.
Shtick.

But a worried look? Why?

I sense myself like crazy. I sense my brain, my spine, my
wings.

Though don't go crazy, "wings." We'll wait on "wings." We'll see.

Will I not fall, like Icarus in the Brueghel, seen and unseen?

I-who-am-Bobby observe the window. I observe the night. I observe the building cornice across the street, and I observe myself observing these things.

My back is to the others now. I've served dinner, what more do they want? They've been well-fed, as they deserve to be. Burps and felicitations, my friends. Now we'll see. If what's what is what's what. I-who-am-Bobby will show them . . . that I can fly.

Sense, run, window, air, shouts, go, leap, go.

Nothing to it now that you're going. Because look, my friends, how time slows.

You thought I was doing this to shorten life, but see how life lengthens. Aren't you, aren't I, surprised?

The air on my hands and face. Calm down. Sense.

You're not really flying yet, you know, you're falling.

But oh so slow, who could really say?

Chilly air up here. Should've worn a scarf. Planning. Forgetful. Next time make a list.

A disputation on time as I-who-am-Bobby fall—or is it fly? And observe myself falling—or is it flying? Between the tenth floor and the ninth all of time in all the cosmogonies ever imagined passes by, I-who-am-Bobby experiences it all, the fires and the ice, the gold and the iron. And how will the time between the ninth and eighth beat that? Beat that, you sucker! Beat all the time that ever was! But somehow, there's even more time now, and more between the eighth and the seventh! Billions and billions of cosmogonies. Cosmogonies never thought.

Get the picture, get the dream? Still on the seventh floor. I long for a break in my fall. Why has the snow stopped falling? I long for a little snow in my face.

No fear. Why fear? When you see how much time you've really got.

On one floor all the animals troop by. It's like Noah, it's like creation. The garden, or excuse me, the Garden. I-who-am-Bobby take a peek. All these windows, some bright, many dark.

Million-stories-in-the-naked-city time. Million stories in the naked city got nothin' on me. Million stories, small potatoes.

What a dream he sent me.

And there's more. All for the $4.95 shipping and handling.

If I-who-am-Bobby wake up will I fall too fast? If I-who-am-Bobby wake up will I miss out?

But I want to wake up! I am here to wake up! Why else was I in this loft, why else am I in this sky, if not to wake up? How could I forget, when self-remembrance is all?

Sixth floor, lingerie. Fifth floor, hats.

I-who-am-Bobby have lived a hundred billion squillionquadrillion light years already, I've lived as many light years as Scrooge McDuck's got money in his bin, and it's all petty cash. What a cartoon. What a story. Hear me out! I can fly!

And the sensation of it is just like life. Look around. Sense. Listen.

On the fourth floor my eyes go inside and the place is empty except for old sewing machines and junk and I go through a door and pretty soon I'm on a road that goes through galaxies of stars. Pretty nifty, no? Just one of the many opportunities. Just one of the things you're missing when you sit there like a lump.

Take a flyer! See the natural wonders! The Zambezi! Victoria Falls! Where space and time come together!

Third floor, colors. Second floor, shapes.

Or, third floor, fire. Second floor, water.

Or third floor, something else. Second floor, something else, a broken record maybe.

Suddenly I wouldn't mind a broken record, a broken record seems just the thing, because I-who-am-Bobby am running out of floors. It's the most awful thing in the world, really, to have lived a godzillion times a hundred billion squillionquadrillion light years and to realize it's almost up, to see the end looming up, rather fast really, like Louie on the sidewalk there, coming up the block.

He doesn't see me. How sad I feel that life is so short. No matter how long it is it's short. And no matter how many times you say that no matter how short it is it's long, when you get to the end of it, it's short.

This is what I-who-am-Bobby am thinking anyway, as I prepare to abandon ship. Throw the switches. Hear the alarms. Dive! Dive! Dive! Get me out of here. I can't fall anymore, I'm finally going to have to fly.

Was it all a lie?

Wings? What about a rocket-powered booster out my ass? Wouldn't that work just as well? A methane-powered universe?

I sense my arms, I sense my wings, I sense my angel's breath. I am they, I am not this falling thing.

Was it all a lie?

I could still live, in a blink of an eye, more quattrobillion-squilliongodzillion light years than I've lived already, but what would be the point? There's still an end coming. There's always an end. I begin to feel totally exhausted, like I haven't slept, not really, in really quite a while. Why fight it? Why put off the inevitable? Let's go, let's move out, angel wings-or-rocket-powered-booster-out-my-ass-or-both-at-once don't fail me now, sense so dearly you sense light itself, become light itself, that will lift you away.

Huh? Say what again? I-who-am-Bobby do a bit of a wry, tragicomic doubletake, like a scientist in a cartoon when he realizes he's got something wrong, the formula's off, back to the drawing board, I-who-am-Bobby say to myself, there can't be so many subjects and objects, there's got to be just . . . dot dot dot. Quick, go with that then, dot dot dot, sense so deeply dot dot dot that dot dot dot . . . whoa, like the last words on a flight recorder before a crash.

Oh fuck.

Was it all a lie?

I woke up then.

CHAPTER 26

PHILIP KNEW THE PARENTS a little bit. When they came to the city once, he'd shown them around the *New Yorker*. They liked Philip. He was low-key, friendly, didn't do that busy, obscure New York stuff; spent the time with them anyway. A demystifier. Philip was always a demystifier. He explained to them as best he could what had happened. They already knew about the group. Bobby, in a proselytizing moment, a moment of high confidence, even pride, or was it defiance, had told them a little. It frightened them, but they weren't surprised.

Bobby's father was one who tried to explain things, to himself, to his wife. She didn't want to hear.

All she wanted to hear was her music, Bach, she had a little cassette player, like a pre-Walkman, that she kept with her and played all the time, as if the Goldberg Variations would drown out the rest.

That was the saddest part, Philip said. Even when he talked to them it was playing, though she turned it down a little. Her eyes were glassy. Philip didn't say to them, when the father asked who Joe was, that he was some weird guru Bobby had gotten mixed up with; because Philip didn't think it was so, and it wasn't. Not in my view, anyway. Not then; nor, really, now either.

*

I'm trying very hard to remember if Philip really said "saddest." I remember quite clearly where we had the conversation, at the coffee shop that used to be at Broadway and Canal that was known for its egg creams. It was some days later. "Sad," "saddest." Not words that Philip used, because to use them was to express negative emotions, to falsify, manipulate, attack. But I know he didn't say it was the "worst" part. Nor the "most difficult" part. Nor the "craziest" part. I'm pretty sure he said the saddest part.

*

If this story could go one way or another, if it could nudge itself, say, in the direction of a movie sale, I suppose there could be a crisis now. Did he jump or was he pushed? Does our Assistant-D.A.-by-accident-or-design believe his friends or suspect them? Does he protect them or betray them? Does he get jammed up himself?
Figure the girl's in it up to her eyeballs.
And there'd have to be evil so that there could be good.
The kinds of movies Joe loved always had lots of both.

*

But the story doesn't nudge itself. The only betrayals, as usual, are the writer's.

*

The family made arrangements to take the body back to Cleveland. There was nothing in the *Times*. I didn't know then, and don't know now, if this was because such a death was not newsworthy on New Year's Day 1979, or because somebody hushed it up. Or it just fell through the cracks. The *Harvard Crimson* reported it. A short piece, that talked about the lamppost on Mount Auburn Street and his contributions to the various Harvard magazines and his successes in New York. Something I didn't know. He'd been invited into the startup of a new *Lampoon* radio show—the one that later lent so much (is this the polite way of putting it?) to the creation of *Saturday Night Live*.

*

At the meeting on Thursday night, everyone came and a bowl of dates was passed. The twenty-nine birds. I got there early to get a seat on a bench. Others with more supple legs folded them on the green carpet. I noticed, beyond the galley, that the window had been fixed. Pristine dunes of white putty bordered glass as clear as rainwater. Otherwise I sensed the disorientation of being in a place that looked the same but was not. Joe made no speech, said nothing at all for awhile. He sat in his Eames chair and smoked his Newports. His face was hard to read, but it seemed maybe swollen, a fighter after a fight. His watery eyes did their usual dance around people's stares. But he didn't seem uncomposed. I surveyed the room. Most of the others were as regular and dispassionate as he. The work was continuing. Was it possible? That people were simply sensing, trying, in the shadow cast by this new development, the loss of someone they might have called their mascot, to deal with whatever might be "coming up" now? Working on themselves.

Was I working on myself?

What the fuck was going on?

It wasn't Joe alone. No one seemed ready to say anything. Ten minutes passed, perhaps more. I hated the crowding on the benches. I hated sensing the heat of others' arms. I told myself not to make words out of these. Sense the sweat of others if you must but why do you have to subvocalize it, lay everything up with illusion? Then told myself not even to tell myself this much, then told myself not to tell myself *that*.

The old joke. The old college try.

But overall, the words in my head may have been less then. Instead of words, snatches of songs. Maisie, Maisie, give me your answer true. I'm half-crazy . . . while Maisie sat there, on the bench to my right, her knees apart, her ashtray in her hand, her red hair like a one-man flag. Joe did not even say "Does anyone have anything they want to talk about?"

It seemed as though we might break up without one thing being said. It had happened two or three times over the course of things, meetings at which people sat there until Joe called it a night. I'd felt each time an embarrassed queasiness, as if open to accusations I could not quite hear, but my discomfort was clearer and fiercer now, and it had the sweaty oppressiveness of shame. Spade whom I wrote for so many hours would say something now. When your friend dies, aren't you supposed to? When your mascot dies . . .

I almost said those words exactly, shame, Spade, mascot. But no wind blew them out of my throat. Maisie, Maisie, give me your answer true.

Or give me anything, the world is out there longing to be kissed or at least seen.

"He said something," I said.

Surprising myself that these words were actually aloud.

As if I scarcely knew where they came from, my voice husky in a room that seemed to dim.

"Who did? Bobby did?"

Joe's radio baritone, easy, reassuring, skimmed over me as if my intention were deeper, buried in a bunker.

Was this really me, speaking so hoarsely, with scarcely a pre-meditated word in sight? "He said, yesterday, he could fly. . . . He said he had to escape. . . . I mean, he said them at different times. It wasn't like they were together. He started talking to me in the liquor store, about flying. I didn't . . . I let it drop, because there was a guy I knew standing near us, I didn't want him to hear . . ."

"So it's all your fault?"

"Is it? He also said . . . he told me we were food, we were already dead, our heads were bitten off."

"Oh? By who?"

"You," I said.

"So then it's my fault."

Which was the kind of thing Joe said often enough, and usually gleefully enough, as if it were child's play. But he was grim now, playing for keeps. His glance arced over our heads on the benches like a missile shot, which then, gathered back by gravity, landed somewhere on the flat neutrality of the elevator doors.

"I didn't mean it that way," I said.

"But it's not your fault, it's my fault," Joe insisted. "That's what you think."

"I don't know . . . if anyone's to blame."

"But you don't want it to be you."

"No."

The boundaries of my skin seemed to thin, so that, sensing myself, I formed a mental image of myself larger than I was accustomed to think was me, I extended more out into the room. I sensed myself more deeply, until my skin seemed to melt into my sensing of it, the two were one and the same, and "I," released from my skin, reached out to the others on the benches, a little bit more, a little bit more, until I felt I could almost grab Joe and make him a part of "me." Later I imagined that what I felt might have been what a person who loses a limb feels, when he can see it isn't there but senses that it still is.

Then it simply ended. Joe was taking a moment, as if he'd won. Maybe he had. His cigarette parked on his lip.

"He almost hit you. He could have landed on you. You'd be dead. Don't you feel a little angry about that part?"

I didn't know what I felt, but I knew that it wasn't anger, and I said nothing.

"Who else thinks it's their fault?" Joe asked.

There coalesced in me then a distinct, even striking, expectation that others would chime in, explaining how it was their fault, it would be everybody's fault, kind of the reverse of the old Pete Seeger song where a boxer dies and everyone who knew him disclaims responsibility. A cheap, heroic Hollywood scene of indictment and catharsis from the black-and-white days when there was such a thing as "the people." My eyes tracked around the benches and I could almost hear what everyone would say. Philip would be chirpy, above

the fray, but confess he had a crush on Bobby and had told him once
and scared him. Joe would remember the time, when Bobby was
complaining about something so trivial that Joe had long since forgotten what it was, that Joe had said to him, jokingly, to get him to
shut up and stop "attacking" him with his little pity-inducing complaints, "Well, you can always jump." Ty would rue firing him off a
magazine job, long ago, for being so late turning anything in. Liddie
wouldn't go out with him. Phyl wouldn't give him a blow job when
he asked and why not because she gave everybody else. Val would
remember dreams where Bobby was a devil. Raoul just plain didn't
like him, for being a show-off, stealing attention. Greg would shed
big sentimental tears for not having eaten Bobby's Peking duck,
for having left it on the plate and Bobby had picked the plate up
and stared at the uneaten portion. Big Ronald never listened to
him, thought he was crazy, never trusted him for having been—
no offense to present company—at Harvard. Julie told him what
to do the whole time in the galley, castrated him left and right,
when she worked with him before me. Laura didn't like his cartoons, they were so violent, Bobby could see her face twist up when
she looked, this was just last week and she was surprised how hurt
he looked. And so it would have gone, the confessions, if that's
what they were, the contributions, as if people were tossing their
bits and pieces on a pyre.

I imagined this scene but it didn't happen.

The only other one who spoke was Maisie.

All she really said was that he was sweet. "He wasn't a 'power-
mad rat,' like some people said. He was sweet."

Her throaty voice, its smoke burying the dead.

She also said that when she dumped him, she gave all the "group" excuses. He was crazy, he was trouble. All the things people said about her.

But she'd been sick and she was here to see Joe, to help her get better, and she was supposed to not need trouble, trouble was supposed to be bad for her health. And so . . . and so . . . "He was sweet, Bobby was a sweet boy," she said.

Maisie, Maisie, all for the love of you.

When Maisie was done, Joe put a leg up and began to play with his toes. His feet were thick like his neck, I remember his black socks then, he rubbed his toes through his black socks as though he was massaging them, warming them up, and it seemed all so much like an act that I felt we were supposed to recognize it as such. Then he started to laugh. It was one of those freak storms that start more suddenly than you think a storm can, a big rolling laugh bouncing off us all, a squall of a laugh, his eyes wet and his belly quaking, a cliché and happy to be one. He let his foot go and stretched his arm out like a cartoon of a Zen master yawning, getting all the laugh that was in him out.

Joe didn't seem to care that no one laughed with him, that he was making a spectacle of himself. It was a laugh big enough that it could have irony in it and still not be ironic, rage in it and not be angry, it subsumed these, put them in their proper places, no more parts of his laugh than they were parts of life.

Joe never made a spectacle of himself but now he did. All of us looked at him with . . . how shall I say this without compounding the mystery of it? Reflections of ourselves? In my case it might have been fear. His laugh lasted more than a minute, it was like an episode, or a seizure, something that you could describe in medical terms. Nor was he laughing to himself. It felt like a code being sent out into the night. When he was done with it, the meeting was over.

As we left I observed Philip at the elevator, like the rest of us saying nothing, slipping on his shoes with what seemed now less like conscious attention, more like the slow weight of years.

*

And what did the laugh mean? I had no idea, but Philip did. We met a second time in the coffee shop at Broadway and Canal, a few days following the Thursday meeting. He said he thought it had to do with, if you join an expedition and you know it's dangerous, then if something happens, if you were Bobby how would you want people to remember you, as a victim? It was sort of like one of those NO ONE UNDER 18 ADMITTED signs, no one under eighteen admitted, and no pity either.

"So we should honor Bobby in his strength, not his weakness?" I actually used such tall, ungainly words.

Philip didn't answer. He stirred his coffee and looked at me oddly. I remembered when I first met him and had observed that he was not afraid to stare at people. I thought maybe he was in a kind of trance. I was also quite sure, despite his words, that he was very angry at Joe.

The reason we met then was that I'd polished up my story about Joao. Philip read it through. When he was done all he said was, "Let's see . . ." He put his coffee aside, laid the five triple-spaced pages flat on the formica between us, and as if I weren't there went through them with the Mont Blanc pen, gilded with his initials, that had been his Christmas present to himself. After awhile there was hardly a phrase of mine that had not suffered at least collateral damage. The pages were crisscrossed with blue trails so ornately and densely patterned that I had hardly an idea what he had written. It took him forty-five minutes. When he was finished, he grinned slightly—a grin, I thought at the time, of grim satisfaction—and said, "Not bad." The way Joe always said it.

The story appeared the following week but by then the Angel of Saint Vincent's had disappeared. No one at the hospital knew what had become of him, though the Puerto Rican nurse who liked having him around thought it must have had to do with the law. I checked this out with Immigration and the NYC police, but neither of those had picked him up. He was simply gone. Did he ever see himself on a newsstand somewhere, or in a magazine left on a bus seat, or in a public library? I don't know.

I felt an odd pride for our story. I recognized in it a few things, for example, the sums that Joao and I had calculated he'd saved the city. Mostly I felt like a stranger to the very things that I'd uncovered. But hadn't I been present at the creation? I felt a little as I'd felt when I copied Hammett. I searched for the verbal formulation that might express the maximum sense of my achievement without outright lying. "I worked with Philip Deschayne on a Talk story." "Philip's been teaching me how to write Talk stories and we just had one in." But really I had no one to tell. This was Philip's world, finally. I thanked him for the way he'd involved me in it and he mumbled some version of "you're welcome," but all our words sounded a little stilted, as if there were echoes of Bobby in them, as though in wanting to make sure we didn't say too little, we were inevitably saying too much. He shared with me the five hundred dollars.

*

It was the end of the group. In three months Joe moved to Berkeley. Some went with him, some stayed.

I stayed. So did the other "intellectuals," we who were there early, the Harvard-Yale types. But Liddie went with him, and Big Ronald and Greg, several of those who came to Joe through his ad in the *Voice*. Maisie returned to Boston.

I stopped doing the morning exercise. The first morning that I determined not to do it I felt "the terror of the situation," as if I'd lost my bearings in the world.

I stopped, also, fighting to "stay present to myself," to "remember myself," I stopped telling myself to "stop, go back, gently."

Yet I seemed to sense myself without telling myself to. A habit I didn't quite care to shake, a talisman maybe, a chip on the luck of life, or a deal brokered with my fear. I could hardly tell, in totality, whether after leaving the group I had more words in my head or less. I judged it all to be about the same. Maybe it had always been the same.

All the time that I was in the group, one strand of my free-floating fantasy had it that I'd liked Philip and Bobby better before there was a "group," that what I really liked about it all was the little literary "salon" at Philip's, the spare poetry of the stories read there, the *Bird Guide*, the *New Yorker*, the pretty pathway for my ambition. In this view, the group was like a fetter, but one necessary in order to enjoy the rest. Now that the bond was gone, it seemed as if life might be wide open, as if I would have everything and eat it too. I quit my job downtown. I went back to writing everyday. But the *Bird Guide* died for lack of a purpose, and Philip soon found himself in a fresh writer's block as big as all of 43rd Street between Fifth and Sixth. Despite the Angel of Saint Vincent's, the *New Yorker* seemed farther away. The battle for Shawn's succession had begun, at least the early skirmishes, and Philip himself began to have contempt for the place. Even the streets of the city, which I had thought would be all mine all the time for prowling and scoring, seemed mostly busy now. I spent a couple weeks on a sexual spree, then tired of it. I began to notice that I had little money.

A last straw of sorts was that the Old Painter started spreading rumors about Joe. Rumors or simply statements of misgiving. I heard these from Joe first. The Old Painter was saying Joe shouldn't have been teaching to start with, he didn't have his blessing to do it, he understood nothing, and Bobby Gelfand should still be alive. I wondered what Maisie had told him. He sounded like an old Jewish patriarch disowning his son.

*

I went out to Los Angeles, moved into an apartment in Ocean Park, and began writing scripts to send around. For twelve hundred dollars I bought an old Cutlass convertible. My tiny apartment had a sliver of an ocean view.

One weekend I drove the Cutlass up to Berkeley. Joe was living in a two story bungalow off Sacramento Street. An assortment of mostly older cars jammed the driveway and the parking places around his house. It was a Sunday morning in the fall. The air lacked any crispness but in distinction to Ocean Park, Berkeley had at least a brave cohort of trees whose leaves dared show their age and turn brown. I went inside the house. The walls were unfinished—or more likely, the sheet rock had been pulled off them—leaving the feeling of a cabin in the woods. Joe's Eames chair sat in the front room a bit regal for its surroundings and there was also a Franklin stove and a stack of futons and benches, the last parked against the wall studs. A familiar green carpet covered the floor. People with fresh, unfamiliar faces waxed the benches, cleared ashes from the stove. One person was washing the small, high-set windows. Everyone worked with self-conscious slowness. It was as if I were watching an old dance performed by a new troupe of players. None of these people appeared to notice me, or they did and refused to be distracted.

Presently Liddie walked in. She certainly did see me, but pretended she hadn't. It seemed to be her job to watch the others. She was acting as if either it was perfectly normal for me to be there or I was a non-person. I said nothing to her but smiled her way. This got me nowhere. She touched the arm of the girl who was sweeping out the stove, lightly, no doubt instructively, but I had no idea why.

I wandered through the bungalow. I noticed that no works of the Old Painter were on any of the walls. In the rustic kitchen all the pots and woks from New York were hung over a new galley stove. This transportation of Bobby's old preserve into a new setting that, as it were, owed him nothing, that could not be imagined even to hold a candle for him, was perhaps the most disorienting view of all. I came out through the kitchen onto a redwood deck that overlooked a backyard scarcely wider than the bungalow but deep. Bamboos filled the back of the yard. Three people were at work thinning the bamboos and raking in-between them. The rest of the yard appeared as a slow motion sculpture garden, figures clipping plants, mowing grass, turning a compost heap, planting what looked to be star jasmine by a trellis, pruning an orange tree that dripped with fruit. Big Ronald sat on the deck steps smoking a cigarette, his white legs sprouting out of shorts that must have been recently bought. When I saw him, I waved. I'd always liked Big Ronald. He looked past me as if I were deck furniture.

So it was true. Somebody must have seen me coming. I was being ignored. Or another way of putting it, I reminded myself, was that these people were working, I was interrupting, and they were try-ing not to be interrupted. I sensed myself like crazy then. I didn't want to be attacked. I wanted to figure out what was going on. My sense of it was that people were engaged in something more than maintaining their attention—even the most severe of us in New York, if an old friend arrived from across the country, might have nodded in greet-ing—and that they considered me some sort of deserter, or weak-ling or disappointment. Of course it was possible that I was. I wasn't in a mood to argue, even with myself.

Liddie came out. This time I wasn't ignored. She spoke to me quietly and with conscious neutrality: "If you want to see Joe, he's in his room." I followed her back inside. I felt like I was following a geisha. We walked up the stairs into a redwood-paneled hall at the end of which was a shut door. I could hear radio noise from within, which as we got closer I realized was football.

Liddie opened the door for me. Joe was sitting alone in front of his old Sony. He was in a butterfly chair which made him look a bit planted, like some overgrown species of melon. The room contained a queen-size bed but was otherwise sparsely appointed. A photo of the dancer from Oakland sat on top of the Sony, apparently some-thing had developed in that department, as it always seemed to, qui-etly, for Joe.

"Pull up a chair," he said. He was so matter-of-fact I might have seen him yesterday. The 49ers were playing the Giants in New Jer-sey, so the game had already started.

I sat with Joe and watched. The Giants were ahead by a touch-down but Joe was rooting for them to die and be buried in an un-marked grave. No transplanted New Yorker residual sports team loyalty for Joe. He was for the Niners all the way. He cursed or cheered on every play, though it was all a bit of an act. He was simply enjoying himself, waiting for Montana to swing into action. "He never does anything till there's two minutes left," Joe assured me.

Liddie brought him up some food. He asked me if I wanted anything. I shared some take-out burrito with him. I was sensing myself without even trying, as had always happened when I was with Joe and afraid, but I wasn't really afraid now. Joe asked me if I liked his place and I said I did. He asked me if I liked Los Angeleeze, his old Bensonhurst way of saying it, and I said I didn't really but that might change if I ever found work. I told him I liked having the beach a couple blocks away. And I told him I found the way others were treating me today a little odd. Like I was a tax collector, or maybe an alien. "Separation anxiety, don't you think?" Joe said curtly. "You were one of their daddies and ran away."

Which made, I supposed, a certain sense; or anyway I flattered myself that it did. I found I still liked it when Joe psychologized, it felt reassuring, a safer port.

"So people haven't been trashing me, or us, in meetings?

"Don't be childish," Joe said.

But I wasn't sure.

Montana rallied his guys in the fourth quarter, completed about fourteen passes, and the Niners won going away. Joe put his leg up and played with his toes and looked self-satisfied. When the game ended, he shut off the set.

I thought maybe it was time for me to leave, but he sat back down.

"So." He pushed out a cigarette and lit it. "We've got people who live in Los Angeleeze who come up here on the weekends. It's not so bad a commute . . ."

"I don't think so," I said.

"If you were ever interested . . ." he continued. "You could probably get a ride . . ."

"Really, I don't think so," I said.

He was silent awhile then. "I've got to go down in a couple minutes. Meeting."

"Of course."

"*Told* you about Montana."

"Yeah."

More silence, more sitting there in the butterfly chairs that turned people into plants. I again got mentally prepared to leave.

"If you're ever in Los Angeles . . ."

"Why would I go to Los Angeleeze?"

I shrugged.

He looked my way with a softer expression. It was mostly in his eyes. They weren't so insistently open, for a moment they lacked that huge belief in themselves. Joe looked, quite possibly, rueful. "Whatever happened in the group," he said, "I hope it won't stop you from finding help somewhere else some day."

These seemed at just that moment the kindest words Joe ever spoke to me. The kindest in their intention, the most generous. Or maybe the only really kind words he ever spoke to me. He said them in his baritone, and they seemed so naked and truthful. Though it wasn't long before I started to wonder. What's "kind," what's "kindest."

I didn't answer him, I didn't think that an answer was called for.

Or perhaps I was made uneasy by his words and simply didn't know what to say.

A little while later I left, feeling cloudy.

*

In the ensuing months and years, I kept track of my old friends from the group, Philip particularly. I was good about calling. Philip got married, had two kids, finally left the *New Yorker* after Tina Brown started her rampage. When I went back I'd see Philip and Joe, and once in a while Ty and Valerie, who stayed together.

I sensed they all went back to versions of their earlier selves; either that, or in moving on, more of their old personalities reappeared. Philip resumed suffering writer's blocks and depressions and a scattered, make-do way with deadlines and money, but also a genuine gentleness in him reemerged, or grew stronger, less encumbered by the war on common feelings fought by the group. He seemed less self-consciously in command of himself or his world, but more genuine, and actually stronger. Philip, a father. Wonderful. Perfect. Seeing the others always made me wonder about myself, whether after the group I had regressed or gone forward. I was never sure. I wondered whether those were even the right words, whether there was an arrow pointed one way or the other that you could say ran through people. One thing I noticed for certain, the slightly preternatural sexual prowess I'd developed, the product, I supposed, of such close monitoring of my body combined with the battering my superego took, began to slip away.

I never asked Philip or Joe or anyone who left the group if they were continuing their spiritual pursuits in an organized way, if they'd joined something else, were following someone else. When I visited Philip in his new office at Columbia, I noticed he'd placed all his old Sufi books on reasonably prominent display behind his typewriter, and that some new ones seemed added to the mix. From these I guessed that he might have resumed his relations with the left brain/right brain guy. But I didn't ask. I didn't really want to know. On occasion he seemed bitter or bemused about Joe, he who'd been closest to Joe of all of us. He'd make a remark, in a sardonic tone, about some rumor he'd heard, some story from California. But he may simply have moved on.

For myself, I'm not much of a joiner and never was, despite what this story might suggest. I nibbled a few times. I'd go to hear Krishnamurti speak in Ojai, under the oak trees, sitting taller than a ninety-year-old had any right to sit, lambasting the gurus, disavowing "followers," offering people their own private chance. And I visited a Zen rabbi on LaBrea in Hollywood and found his cheery lox-and-bagel syncretism excruciating.

Instead I read books. Some of the usual suspects and some more obscure, trying to figure out not so much what I might do as what I had already done. Where was I? Where were any of us? When I read a book, say, by Suzuki, I tried to sense myself so deeply that the book would resonate in parts of myself that I scarcely knew were there. But how could I tell the imaginary from the real? An armchair general, some questions I was a little bit content not to be able to answer.

*

It was in the early nineties that I received a letter from Joe. It was a form letter, xeroxed, addressed to "members of my old group." In it Joe said he wanted us to know that he had been wrong about many things in his teaching, chief among them the mixing of psychological concepts with ideas from a different plane of learning altogether, to the confusion of both. He apologized, asked our forgiveness, implied that his failings were due to the fact that the Old Painter hadn't instructed him properly, and requested that if any of us knew someone who had not received this letter, that we send it to him.

He also recommended a book, one I'd never heard of, if we wanted an exposition of certain ideas in keeping with what Joe now understood them to be.

I ordered the book from a secondhand shop and then let it sit on my shelf for a month. When I read it finally, I felt disappointed, even insulted. The book seemed so crude. It assumed the form of an objective description of self-observation and self-remembrance, but it was so larded with tall tales of quasi-miracles and small moments of simple improbability that the author came off as scheming and unreliable, as if he believed himself to be writing from such a lofty perch of spiritual superiority that it entitled him to con the poor peons who'd be reading him, supply them with whatever they might need in order to be impressed, all for the greater good, of course. I'd sometimes detected similar notes in Gurdjieff's own writings, and in the writings of his early followers, as if they were daring you to disbelieve, presenting lies so that you would experience what it is like to be lied to. But perhaps that assigns too great, or too mean, a motive to all of them. In all events, I was embarrassed that Joe had recommended the book.

And it infuriated me that someone in whom I had put so much trust could have slipped so badly. It reminded me of the thing I'd always most doubted about him: his taste. Yet what I remembered about Joe was so much better than the humorous drivel, the clumsy manipulations, of this book. Joe was a magnificent mongrel who took from here and there and didn't care. He was bold, of Brooklyn and America, he didn't kowtow to getting every dot and jot of some dead Armenian's theory right. "Wrong about many things" and proud of it—that was the Joe I remembered, who seemed so absent from his letter.

At the same time, I remembered Bobby's asparagus pee. As well, it's always flattering to be apologized to, especially when the apology comes from one who sometimes bullied you. For a while I was going to write him back, or go up to Berkeley, to tell him I liked the old Joe better, damn the torpedoes and full speed ahead, don't let the bastards get you down. But I didn't like the smell of what he was involved with now, it smelled musty, of texts and ghosts.

I had no one to forward Joe's letter to, Philip had received it and Cal had received it, and by now these were the only two from the group that I was in contact with, so I put it away in a drawer.

*

I bought a house with a rose garden. The roses were of the old varieties, with names as heavily scented as their petals—Duchesse de Brabante, Souvenir de la Malmaison, La Reine Victoria—that have more recently made a return to fashion. Those were busy times for me, but I would try to make room for the roses. On Sunday afternoons you might see me out there, in a wool black-and-orange N.Y. Giants hat too hot for the sun, with a Swiss clippers not unlike Joe's that I doted on a bit, kept cleaned and oiled anyway, and kept indoors.

The woman I bought the house with, who would later be my wife, thought I was less than fastidious with the roses and in some respects this was true. I skimped on the heavy work, the garden always needed more weeding. But actually I liked it pleasantly overgrown.

What I did not tell my future wife, for fear it might be lost in the revelation, was the secret I brought to this amateur's work. As I clipped and shaped, removed deadheads, sprayed for aphids, I made a conscious effort, whenever I noticed there were words in my head, to stop, and go back, gently, to looking, to listening, and to sensing my arms and legs. For moments my mind would be still. I heard the groaning and heaving of the traffic stream on the nearby street, the tinkling of the pool fountain, the jostling songs of the finches at the feeder. I saw the hundreds of shades of rose, the aphids living their lives on the undersides of leaves, the dew, the magical forests of yellow stamens, the warlike plenitude of thorns, as if sufficient to defend whole worlds. I sensed my body so deeply it seemed to be not all of me, but a burning image of me. Peace. I sensed peace.

Inevitably I clipped a rose or bent it towards me and with a relaxed abdomen, from as deep a place as I could find, breathed slowly, unstintingly in, as if I'd discovered a thirst I never knew I had. The perfume of the rose, familiar but scarcely describable, transported me at once out of what seemed the anteroom of my life to the place and time when Bobby Gelfand was alive, we all were young, and eternity seemed possible. Live every minute, the old guy said, in the awareness that one day you will die. I'd hardly done that. I've hardly done that. Joe waddles around his apartment or the loft in his corduroy pants, squirting his miniature roses under their Gro-lites with water from his plastic bottle. We do our work. Bobby's at the stove, cooking something good. Sense. Look. Listen. Thirty birds set off to find the mighty Simurgh, whose name means thirty birds. And how many arrived?